Five friends have fun and adventures

T. M. Alexander likes writing in the morning and sleeping in the afternoon. She does all her plotting while she swims up and down the lake. Her favourite pudding is chocolate anything and her worst pudding is fruit.

Find out more at www.tmalexander.com

Get to know the Tribers at
www.tribers.co.uk

Other Tribe books:
The Day the Ear Fell Off
A Thousand Water Bombs
Labradoodle on the Loose

T M Alexander

Monkey Bars and Rubber Ducks

TRIBE Five friends have fun and adventures

PICCADILLY PRESS • LONDON

For trusty Bod.

First published in Great Britain in 2011
by Piccadilly Press Ltd,
5 Castle Road, London NW1 8PR
www.piccadillypress.co.uk

Text copyright © T.M. Alexander, 2011

A catalogue record for this book is available from the British Library.

ISBN: 978 1 84812 158 4 (paperback)

1 3 5 7 9 10 8 6 4 2

Printed in the UK by CPI Bookmarque, Croydon, CR0 4TD
Cover design by Patrick Knowles
Cover illustration by Sue Hellard

Mixed Sources
Product group from well-managed
forests and other controlled sources
www.fsc.org Cert no. TT-COC-002227
© 1996 Forest Stewardship Council
FSC

Keener
Bunks Off

Late For Lunch

It was sausage and mash for school lunch – result! I turned round to start off a Tribe handshake (only really meant for great triumphs) but after I slapped down my hand, only three others followed . . . when there should have been four. I stopped my other hand in mid-flight.

'Where's Copper Pie?'

Bee's head, Fifty's head and Jonno's head all turned to look behind. There was Alice, and behind her Marco and Ed. But no Copper Pie.

'He must *be* here. He's not exactly going to miss lunch, is he?' said Bee.

'Same,' said Fifty.

They were right. Copper Pie *never* skips a meal. In fact he has extra snacks in between to ensure his stomach is never less than half full.

'Maybe he snuck in early,' said Jonno.

On Tuesdays we have to wait until last to go in for dinner. It's a killer. I scanned the tables to see if our redheaded friend was already munching . . . No.

The thump took me by surprise. It was right in the middle of my back. I lurched forwards and nearly crushed a Year 3 (easily done).

'Sorry,' I said to the Year 3, before I turned round to face my out-of-breath friend, 'What did you do that for?'

'Sorry, Keener. Couldn't stop in time,' said Copper Pie. 'I smelt the sausages.' (Pant. Pant.) 'Didn't want to miss out.'

'Where were you?' said Fifty.

Copper Pie didn't answer, because someone else did.

'He was somewhere he shouldn't have been,' said Callum. He walked towards us with a knowing look on his face.

We don't like Callum, and he doesn't like us. We helped him once, not because we wanted to but because we had to. It didn't change a thing. If Tribe was a ruling pary, Callum and Jamie would be the opposition. No question.

'Go away, Hog,' said Copper Pie.

'Why? Got something to hide?' said Callum.

'No,' said Copper Pie. He stepped so close to Callum, he was nearly treading on the toes of his trainers. 'I just don't like you.'

It looked like trouble, but thankfully Alice – the most

irritating girl in the class, except on this one occasion – decided to get involved.

'You've jumped the queue, Callum. Get to the back or I'll tell . . .' She looked around for a teacher. 'I'll tell Mr Morris.'

'Go ahead. I'll tell him Copper Pie pushed in too, and we can carry on with our little chat at the back, on our own.' Callum was definitely up for a fight.

'You're wrong there,' said Bee. 'Copper Pie was here all the time. Wasn't he, Tribers?'

There was general nodding. I don't really like lying but . . . Callum looked at Alice. Behind her, I could see Mr Morris walking our way.

'But he wasn't, was he, Alice?'

Alice stared straight back at him . . . and nodded, slowly. *Go Alice!* She's not a Triber (and never could be), but she'd stood up for us. *We could try to be a bit nicer to her,* I thought. *Except that she's the most annoying girl, times a million – so maybe not.*

Callum curled his lip, like a villain in an old film, said, 'I'll be watching you,' and disappeared to the back of the line.

'What was that all about?' said Jonno.

We all looked at Copper Pie.

'Is it all right if I get my sausages first?' he said.

We sat at our favourite table in the corner.

'Go on then, spill the beans,' said Bee.

'I think Callum saw me coming through the gates.'

No big deal, I thought. Copper Pie must have wellied the ball right out of the school grounds. It happens regularly. We're not allowed to set a foot outside the perimeter without permission, but no one ever asks. They just dash out, and dash back in.

'He won't tell on you,' said Bee. 'It's not worth it.'

'Same,' said Fifty.

'Depends how much he saw,' said Copper Pie.

Jonno laughed. 'Why? Did you do a quick raid on the café while you were there? Did you nick a hot chocolate?'

I laughed too. But Copper Pie stayed deadly serious.

'What is it?' said Bee, flicking her black fringe out of her eyes to give him her best stare.

'Callum was outside the gates too, getting his ball.' Copper Pie paused.

'And?' said Bee.

'And he might have seen me coming from the alley.' Copper Pie winced.

It was very confusing. Why would Copper Pie be coming out of the alley between end of morning school and last sitting when he should have been in the playground? I hadn't seen him, but I'd assumed he was practising in goal. He often does.

'But where *had* you been?' said Fifty.

'I bunked off,' said Copper Pie. I gasped. This was bad. In fact, worse than bad. He carried on. 'There was something I had to do. And the trouble is, I've got to do it again tomorrow, and the next day . . .'

I had no idea what the 'something' was but I could see what was coming. It was going to be another problem for Tribe to sort out. Why we couldn't have a few normal days being normal children, I didn't know. But one of the Tribers was in a fix, and that meant we were all in a fix. I waited, with a bit of a worry growing inside, to hear the details.

The Details

All sausage eating stopped. All eight eyes were trained on Copper Pie. He took a breath.

'I kicked my football over the fence last night.' He paused. We all willed him to hurry up but no one said anything out loud. He started again.

'Usually Big Jim shouts at me from his kitchen when I go and get it. He sits by the window a lot, watching the birds. He has lots of birds because he puts up those feeders and fills them with peanuts. I sometimes steal a couple.' Copper Pie paused again. This story was going to take a lot of telling.

'He usually says things like, "Get out of my garden, you redheaded layabout". Or he calls me Tomato-head, or Robin . . . but it's a joke.'

He does, and it is. I can remember the first time I heard Copper Pie's neighbour shouting. I was waiting in the garden, with Copper Pie's brother Charlie, for the ball to be chucked back over. I don't know exactly what Big Jim said, because I was too shocked by how loud his voice was, but I know that Copper Pie shouted back, 'Shut up, you grumpy old man', and then there was loads of laughing. I still don't get the joke but Copper Pie and Big Jim are rude to each other all the time and that's how it is.

'I got my ball from over by the hedge, and on the way back I went right by his window. His car was out the front, so I knew Big Jim must be in. He's too old to walk very far.' There was a big pause. So big that Fifty started eating his sausage. So big that Copper Pie had to be nudged into action.

'What did you see?' said Bee. 'What did you see through the window?'

I leant forward in my chair. Jonno pushed his glasses right up to the top of his nose. Fifty took another bite.

'I saw Big Jim,' said Copper Pie. 'He was on the floor.'

Bee made an I'm-shocked noise and put her hand over her mouth. All I could think was *blood*. Fifty swallowed and spoke for all of us.

'Copper Pie, please, please could you tell the story without all the gaps because we'd like to know whether your neighbour was dead, and if not, what your neighbour lying on the floor has to do with you bunking off. And if possible we'd like to know before the afternoon bell goes.' Fifty used a posh voice and a pleading face and pressed his hands together to make pleading hands.

'I'll try,' said Copper Pie. 'The back door wasn't locked – never is – so I went in. I thought he was unconscious, you know, in a coma, but he spoke as soon I got in. He said, "Can you give me a hand, Pumpkin-head?"' (Copper Pie rolled his eyes.) 'I asked him if I should get Mum but he said "NO" – and he really meant it. So I helped him up, which was like lifting a . . . yeti.'

'A sack of potatoes is what people usually say,' I said.

'Shut up, Keener, or we'll never get to the end,' said Bee. I shut up.

'Anyway, I got him into the armchair and that's when I noticed all the other things that were wrong.' (*Oh no!* I thought. *This is where we get the blood and gore.*) 'There was a brown puddle on the floor with two wet Bourbon biscuits, a broken mug, and the cat's bowl was turned over and there was cat food everywhere, but no cat.'

'Was it rabbit poo in a tasty stew?' asked Fifty. Stupid thing to say considering we were trying to hurry the story up. That's Fifty for you.

'Shut up, Fifty. This is serious.' Bee did the glare.

Fifty did a sorry face. 'Go on, Copper Pie,' he said.

'Anyway, it turns out Big Jim had fallen out of the tree on Saturday. He was filling the bird feeder and he slipped off the chair he was standing on. He went to hospital. It must have been when we were out or Mum would've noticed.

He's got a bandage on his arm and he's broken his ribs. And Carlotta – that's the cat – had disappeared, cos she was hungry.' Copper Pie leant right back so that his chair was balanced on two legs. He seemed to have finished. We all looked at each other.

'So do we need to find the cat? Staple posters to all the lampposts with a photo?' said Bee. 'Organise a search party like we did when Doodle was lost.'

I wished she hadn't said that. I still feel guilty about losing her dog, even though Doodle ended up having a lovely sleepover at the café.

'No. The cat came back while I was there. Must have heard me open the tin.' (Quite funny for C.P. – he's not very witty.) 'It was turkey and something.'

'Copper Pie, it's very sad for Big Jim, but what's it got to do with you coming out of the alley at lunchtime?'

I was glad Bee had asked. I didn't want to in case the answer was obvious to everyone else but me. I concentrated on my sausages for a bit.

'You went to see him, didn't you?' said Jonno.

C.P. nodded. *Trust Jonno to work it out*, I thought.

'Couldn't you have waited till after school?' said Fifty.

'He needed his lunch,' said Copper Pie.

'Since when have you been Meals on Wheels?' Fifty laughed, but Copper Pie didn't.

'Since now,' he said.

None of it was making sense. There are social workers

11

and nurses who look after people who are hurt. Why was Copper Pie doing it? It's not as though he was qualified. Imagine the advert in the paper:

ONE GINGER-HAIRED BOY,
GOOD AT FOOTBALL AND
FILLING HIS FACE, BAD
AT EVERYTHING ELSE,
REQUIRED FOR HOME HELP.

As if!

'But why you, Copper Pie?' said Jonno. 'Doesn't he have a family?'

'Nope, no family. But he told the doctors he did. That's why they let him come home.'

Fifty stepped in. 'Copper Pie, can you try to tell the story without any gaps? If you say it all at once, rather than in bits, we might understand.'

'I'm trying, OK!' Copper Pie swung his chair forwards and the front legs made a loud bang. 'He told the hospital his daughter would look after him, but it was a lie. He doesn't have a daughter. But he said if they knew he was all on his own they wouldn't have let him out. They'd have put him in a home.' The situation was becoming clearer. 'He said, "I'd rather be dead than stuffed in a home with a load of dribbling idiots watching *Antiques Roadshow* and looking around for their dead pets."' A picture of an old lady stroking a stuffed cat with a sticking-up tail and glass eyes popped into my head.

'So *you're* looking after him?' said Bee, sounding as though it was close to being the worst thing in the world.

'Don't look at me like that. What else was I meant to do? One arm doesn't work so he can't make any food. And it hurts him to bend down so he can't feed the cat. He can't even open a tin. The half a tin that was left in the fridge ended up on the floor cos it hurt so much when he tried to bend over.'

'Why didn't you ask your mum to help?' said Fifty. (Fifty's mum would be in there like a shot, making healthy food and preparing him herbal tea while she did a bit of reflexology on his big toe to make him relax. She's good at looking after people. Copper Pie's mum wouldn't be quite so good but I'm sure she'd at least give him a jam sandwich and a beaker of squash, like she does with the nursery kids.)

'I wanted to, but Big Jim said my mum would feel she had to call social services, and they'd take him away. I can't tell anyone.'

'Except us,' said Jonno.

'But what can we do?' said Bee. 'I mean, Callum's already clocked you. It's only a matter of time before he catches you if you go every day and then the Head'll have the perfect excuse to get rid of you.'

Copper Pie shrugged, picked up his fork and ate his sausages, whole. We did the same, except we cut them up and chewed.

What a mess, I thought. *But at least it's nothing to do with me.*

'There's only one thing for it,' said Jonno. 'Tribe'll have to help out. If Callum's going to be spying on Copper Pie, let him. One of us can go and feed Big Jim and his cat instead.'

No way, I thought. Being a Triber was the best thing in my life but that didn't mean I'd agree to being a truant. Nope, not me.

Same

It was Tuesday afternoon, which means science and then D.T. We did photosynthesis in science. It's completely straightforward but there are always stupid questions, usually from Alice. And if not, Jamie (Callum's sidekick). This week it was both.

Alice's hand went up first. 'Miss Walsh, do plants eat three meals a day, like we do, or all the time?'

She doesn't really think plants eat three times a day. She says things like that for attention. I immediately changed my mind about being nicer to her for being on Copper Pie's side in the lunch queue.

Jamie's question was slightly more sensible: 'What does the plant do if there isn't no sun?' But he shouted out instead of putting his hand up so we all had to listen to our teacher explaining the rules, again!

And then she said, 'Does anyone want to tell Jamie the answer?'

I knew it, but I didn't want to say so. I'm already called Keener, I don't need to make it more obvious by being even keener – if you get me.

Jonno did his version of putting his hand up, which makes him look like he's bidding in an auction. One finger goes up for a second and that's it.

'Plants store some energy to use when there isn't enough sunshine.'

'That's right. Well done, Jonno.'

Miss Walsh put Jonno's name on the board in the column with the smiley face at the top, under Bee's. (She was up there because she did a mime in P.E. of trying to walk a disobedient dog. Miss Walsh said it was good, but as Bee's dog *is* a disobedient dog it wasn't that hard.) No one was in the sad-face column. Yet.

On the way to D.T. Callum caught up with us.

'So, are you bunking off again tomorrow, Copper Pie?' said his voice from right behind us. 'Off to the arcade?'

So, Callum thought Copper Pie had left school to play on the slot machines. I turned to look at him. So did the others, all except Copper Pie. He kicked his leg out backwards, really hard, and got Callum on the kneecap with the back of his black Adidas trainer. (He's picky about his trainers.) It made a clunk on impact.

THINGS TRIBERS ARE PICKY ABOUT

COPPER PIE: His trainers (Adidas, black tops, black soles, black laces).

FIFTY: His hair, he likes his curls bouncy (it makes him look taller).

KEENER: His glue, it has to stick well but not be too sticky.

BEE: Her food, organic and chemical-free (opposite of C.P.'s diet).

JONNO: His friends, obviously. Why else would he have chosen Keener, Fifty, Copper Pie and Bee when he was a new boy?

'Sorry, Hog! Didn't see you there.'

I hate it when there's fighting. There's always a chance someone might hurt me.

Callum bent over and his blond hair flopped over his face. I think he might have been hiding watery eyes. After a bit, he wiped his face and looked up.

'I know, you're up to something. I'm watching you, Ginger.' He swivelled to include the rest of the Tribers. 'I'm watching *all* of you.'

'Let us know if we drop anything,' said Jonno.

Callum sneered at Jonno and walked off.

'Well, that's great,' said Fifty. 'We're planning on bunking off and Callum's planning on spying. Excellent!'

We all shut up.

In D.T. I couldn't concentrate. We were going to get caught, I knew it. How could one of us go and help Big Jim every lunchtime with Callum sniffing around?

I was meant to be making a gas mask holder, part of the evacuee stuff in history, but it was going nowhere. I usually like D.T., but all I wanted to do was figure out a way to help Big Jim without having to leave the school grounds in the middle of the day. Bunking off was a crazy idea. Tribes are meant to stick together, hunt as a pack. Splitting up would leave us open to predators like Callum and Jamie, or worse, teachers. We needed to learn from the Three Musketeers, 'all for one and one for all'. They didn't all go off in different directions and hope for the best. (At least I don't think they did.)

WHAT I KNOW ABOUT THE THREE MUSKETEERS

- There were four of them – they started off as three but then d'Artagnan joined (Bit like Jonno joining us.)
- They were good at swordfights
- They laughed a lot
- They all had long hair

> • They always won
> • They always said, 'All for one and one for all', just before they annihilated the enemy

After the bell, Jonno and Bee went off to meet Bee's mum. Doodle had an appointment at the vet's. Why Jonno was going too, I don't know. (I know Jonno likes Doodle, but he likes me too and he doesn't come to the doctor's with me.) Copper Pie ran off saying he promised to get Big Jim some grapefruits – he says he likes them for breakfast. So that left me and Fifty to walk home together.

I waited for him to say something about the bunking off plan. I knew he would. He gets as worried as I do about trouble, but when we're all together he relies on me to be the one to say it out loud. When it's just the two of us he's a lot wimpier.

'I don't think Jonno's idea makes sense. We can't look after an old man. We're kids. I mean, what if something happened to him? It would be our fault.' That's what he said. What he meant was that he was scared stupid about bunking off.

'I think we should tell someone,' I said. What I meant was I was scared stupid about bunking off too. It's helpful if you can read your friend's thoughts.

'Same,' said Fifty.

I felt a whole lot better after that. We kicked a stone most of the way to Craven Road. We might have got it all the way to Fifty's road but I took my eye off it when Marco appeared from nowhere and nearly ran us down.

'Hey, Keener! Hey, Fifty!' he shouted as he raced past. I recognise the sound of his mountain board wheels now, but I still can't react in time. Marco's OK. I wasn't sure about him when he first came to our school because he was always shouting in Portuguese. He shouts in English now, which is way better.

Just before the corner where we go in different directions Fifty said, 'So who do you think we should tell?'

I'd been thinking about that. 'No idea,' I said.

'Same,' said Fifty.

'But it's not up to us anyway,' I said. 'Tribe can decide.'

'Same.' If I had one wish I'd make it impossible for Fifty's mouth to say 'same'. (No I wouldn't. It'd be a waste.)

KEENER'S WISHES

- To be a surf champion living in Hawaii
- To trade in his two sisters for computer games
- To have a face that doesn't go pink at the slightest embarrassment
- To be a Triber forever
- To win the lottery without buying a ticket
- To win anything without buying a ticket

Keener Bunks Off

> - To vaporise Callum
> - To have a special power, like flying, or time travel
> - To have Jonno's bedroom

'See you tomorrow, then,' I said. In my head it all seemed sorted. The Tribers would realise we couldn't sneak off with Callum (and probably Jamie too) watching our every move. They'd agree we'd have to tell someone. Between us, we'd think of someone we could trust to look after Big Jim, *and* not tell the old-people snatchers.

I couldn't think of anyone but that didn't worry me. There had to be someone.

Wednesdays

I like Wednesdays because we have the weekly Tribe meeting at six o'clock (that's after tea for me but before tea for Jonno because his family eat at, like, bedtime). The Tribehouse we built at the bottom of Fifty's garden is looking really good. We get into the garden through the cat flap Fifty's dad made for us in the fence – saves going through the house. We've got a shelf and a bench as well as the safe, which doubles as Fifty's seat. There's a photo of us all in our wetsuits drawing-pinned to the wall and a sign saying *Tribehouse* that Flo made because she felt guilty about all the fuss she made over Jack's lost medals. (I can't be bothered to explain. It's all over now.)

I feel like I've been a Triber forever, but it was only when Jonno joined at the beginning of the summer term that it all happened. Before that we were just mates — me, Bee, Copper Pie and Fifty. Now we've got our rituals: fist of friendship and Tribe handshake, our rules — can't leave and can't join, and a safe full of Tribe stuff, like our Fact Files. And we've even got fans. There are loads of kids that would like to be a Triber. Even my dad wants to join! Tribe is ace.

But this Wednesday didn't start very well at all. By the time Fifty and I got to school the others were already huddled together on our patch by the netball courts. And as we got nearer I heard Bee's voice.

'Let's wait for the others to get here and then we'll decide whose turn it is today.'

No, no, no, I thought. *Fifty and me have decided we need to tell someone about Big Jim. The plan's changed.* Sometimes it seems like the others can read my thoughts, but they obviously couldn't this time . . .

'Keener, Fifty, we need to decide who's going to go over to Big Jim's today. Copper Pie's told him to expect one of us. And he's explained why.'

Copper Pie stopped eating his crisps (which are meant for break) and spoke, 'Jim gave me some tips for losing our tail.'

'What tail?' said Fifty, looking over his shoulder for his imaginary tail.

'He means Callum,' said Bee. 'Jim reckons if Copper Pie looks suspicious — you know, keeps looking around and acting weird — then Callum will concentrate on him, leaving one of us free to —'

It was too much. I had to try and put a stop to it.

'Fifty and I have got another idea.' Everyone looked at me, except Fifty who looked at the floor. That was so typical. I was fed up with being labelled as the wimp so I nudged him. 'Don't try and pretend you don't agree.'

'Sorry,' he said.

'Agree with what?' asked Jonno. 'Sorry for what?'

I was about to explain but Fifty did it instead. *Makes a change.*

'Keener and I were talking on the way home last night and we decided it was risky to leave Big Jim all day with only a quick check on him at lunchtime. We decided that if something happened to him it would be our fault for not telling an adult. So we think we should abandon the plan for Tribe to look after him and tell someone who we can trust not to tell anyone else. That would be more responsible.'

'Find me a bucket, someone. You two make me sick. What you mean is, you and Keener are too chicken to bunk off, even to help an old man who'll die if he's sent to a home where they drug you to make you sleep all day and don't feed you.' Copper Pie was hopping mad. And worse, he was right.

Bee's reaction was just as bad. 'We're not doing it for a laugh. We're doing it because he *needs* us.'

Jonno joined in. 'Listen, Copper Pie didn't get caught yesterday, did he? We won't get caught either, because we'll all look out for each other, because we're Tribe.'

'And he's expecting someone,' said Copper Pie. 'So someone's got to go.' Copper Pie stared at me.

I looked away. If I had to play truant I was going to need a few days (at least) to summon up the courage. If I went last it wouldn't be me till Monday, five days. Maybe by Monday, Big Jim would be better. I decided to ask Mum how long broken ribs and sprained arms, or whatever it was, took to heal.

'Shall we toss a coin to decide who's going today?' said Bee.

'No need. I'll go,' said Jonno. *Hurrah for Jonno!*

'OK. I'll go tomorrow then,' said Bee. *Hurrah for Bee!* 'So, Keener, you're Friday, we can share the weekend, and Fifty, you're Monday.'

'OK,' said Fifty.

No! Not OK! I opened my mouth to say something . . . but Bee swung her fringe out of her eyes and gave me a killer look. I closed it again.

'Great,' she said. 'So this is the plan. Jonno, you'll need to eat your lunch really fast, otherwise you won't get there and back before afternoon lessons.'

'Can do,' said Jonno. 'I'm sure no one'll see me leaving, there's so many people going in and out for lunch, but coming back when everyone's in the playground might be more tricky.'

'Exactly,' said Bee. The bell went but she ignored it. 'So, we need to create a diversion. If we assume you'll be back . . . about ten minutes before end of break?' She looked at Copper Pie. He nodded. 'We'll make sure Callum is concentrating on us.'

'And Jamie,' added Fifty.

All the other kids were lining up, but Bee was running the show and she hadn't finished yet.

'Yes, and Jamie. So, the main thing is to keep an eye on Callum *and* Jamie, and they'll both probably be keeping an eye on us so that should be easy.'

I thought she was done so I moved my left foot forwards, but then Jonno started speaking, so I hovered on one foot for a bit trying to work out if it was a short speech or a long one.

'I think you should all go in different directions after lunch,' he said. I put my foot back down. It was going to be a long speech. 'More chance of keeping Callum and Jamie busy, less chance of them working out I'm missing.'

'Good idea,' said Bee. She looked over her shoulder. The whole school was lined up except us. 'Time to go, then, Tribers.' I picked my foot back up. Copper Pie pushed past me (accidently . . . I think, although he was pretty cross about us trying to get out of helping) and I nearly fell.

I was right at the back of the line. I watched the little kids parade past, while I waited for it to be Year 6's turn. I already had a lump in my throat the size of Sweden. By the time it got to lunchtime it would be the whole of Scandinavia. *If I was this nervous about Jonno bunking off, how was I going make myself do it?*

26

Jonno's Turn

Operation Jonno Feeds Big Jim didn't start off very well.

Last lesson before lunch was deadly dull. I wasn't really listening. I kept looking across at Jonno, wondering if he was nervous. He never looks nervous or worried. In fact he always looks the same – calm, the opposite of me. He doesn't go pink when he's embarrassed, or stop breathing when there's a crisis.

Miss Walsh was explaining the homework that she wanted us to do, which meant it was nearly the end at last. She looked up and said, 'That reminds me. We need two people from this class to join representatives from the other Year 6 class to discuss events for the Year 6 Leavers' Week. Let me see, what about Lily and . . . let's have Jonno. Stay behind for a minute will you? Everyone else, skedaddle.' She grinned. Her attempts at sounding jokey are lame.

We all made the usual racket, dragging our chair legs back at speed to get out of our seats and into the lunch queue before getting caught in the classroom door bottleneck. I shrugged at Jonno as I went past. He did an eye-roll. Bee, Fifty and Copper Pie were ahead of me.

'Typical,' said Bee. 'The one day —'

She stopped. Callum was right behind us.

'What was that?' he said.

'I wasn't talking to you and you know it,' said Bee.

Callum smiled. 'Where are you lot off to today then? The arcade? Or the café?'

'We thought, perhaps, the museum,' said Jonno, appearing from nowhere. He'd escaped from Miss Walsh pretty quickly. 'Do you want to come?' I love the way Jonno does that (not the appearing from nowhere, the sounding like he's being polite when he isn't).

'Ha ha,' said Callum.

Callum stayed in the line, sandwiched between Jonno and the rest of us, so we couldn't talk. It was pasta with a lumpy, runny sauce. I opted for a jacket potato. Finally, we managed to get to a table away from our stalker.

'Scoff, Jonno,' said Copper Pie. 'Jim'll be waiting.'

'I know, I know,' said Jonno, between mouthfuls. 'Tell me again what I have to do when I'm there, while I finish this.'

'He can talk, you know,' said Copper Pie.

'I know, but —'

Maybe Jonno was nervous, I thought. The rest of us know Big Jim, because he's always lived by Copper Pie, but Jonno's never met him.

'OK. Go through the gate into the back garden and in the back door. He'll be sitting in the chair. Make him a hot drink and something to eat, and ask if there's anything else he wants. Get back here, swifto.'

It sounded straightforward. Jonno put in his last forkful.

'But what if your mum sees him?' said Fifty to Copper Pie. I hadn't thought of that. She's next door looking after the nursery kids all day.

Copper Pie shrugged. 'She never leaves the house in the day. Ever.'

Jonno stood up.

'I'll take your tray,' I said. He nodded, and scarpered, still chewing. And that was the beginning of half an hour of torture. Until Jonno was safely back in the school playground, I knew I wasn't going to be able to concentrate on anything. The others chatted as normal, and I just sat. So did Callum, watching us from his table. I couldn't eat all my lunch – swallowing was like squeezing a brick down a straw, so Copper Pie helped out.

'Right, then,' said Bee. 'Shall we go and make ourselves hard to keep track of?'

We all followed Bee's instructions. Copper Pie went to kick a ball about by the goal. Fifty and I went to our patch

– the smelly, damp triangle with the rotting tree stump between the netball courts and the tree, aka Tribe territory. Bee went to chat to Lily in the playground. I could see Callum – he was standing by the doors, watching. His eyes were flicking between our three locations. But I couldn't see Jamie.

'There's Jamie,' said Fifty, reading my mind. He appeared out of the door, and took a position by Callum's side.

'Do you think they'll notice Jonno's not here?' I said.

'Not if we follow Bee's plan,' said Fifty. At that exact moment Bee made the agreed signal – shouting my name. 'Keener!' Everyone in the whole school must have heard.

'OK, off I go,' I said. I went over to where Bee and Lily were. Copper Pie went to the loo, which meant he had to go through the door Callum was guarding. Fifty stayed on our patch. The idea was that if we kept moving, and disappearing indoors, Callum and Jamie would be so busy keeping tabs on us they wouldn't think to check the school gates, which are over the other side of the school, and they wouldn't realise Jonno was missing.

So far so good. The next change of location was planned for when Copper Pie came out of the door. We waited. And waited. Callum was waiting too. You could tell by the way he was fidgeting. He kept pushing the arms of his sweatshirt up and then rolling them down again. I was trying not to stare, but my eyes kept being drawn to the spot. Where was Copper Pie?

'What do you think Copper Pie's doing?' I asked Bee.

'No idea.'

The waiting went on and on. Eventually, after what seemed like ten minutes, Callum spoke to Jamie who then disappeared back through the door.

'Jamie's gone to find Copper Pie, I reckon,' I said to Bee.

'What shall we do?' That was strange coming from Bee. She's the one who always tells us what to do.

'Nothing?' I said.

'We can't do nothing, idiot. If Jamie goes wandering round the school looking for Copper Pie he might spot Jonno coming back. We need to keep them focused on the playground.' She was almost shouting at me.

I put my head in my hands. He was going to be caught. I knew it.

'Thank goodness.'

I took my head out of my hands to see why Bee was thanking goodness. Jamie was back. Good! But there was still no Copper Pie.

I looked over to the netball court where Fifty was standing all on his own under the trees, the only Triber on the Tribe patch. He made 'come here' movements with his hands. It looked like he was rolling pastry, but luckily I know him well enough to decipher his mimes.

'Let's go and see what Fifty thinks,' I said to Bee.

'You go,' she said. 'I'm thinking.'

I looked at my watch on the way across the playground

– seven minutes until the bell. All I wanted was for my four friends to be hanging about on our patch with me, doing nothing more interesting than watching the tree stump for signs of Jonno's friend, the stag beetle who lives there. Why we were always about to get in trouble, in trouble already, or trying to get out of trouble, I didn't know. Before Tribe, I was never in a scrape, ever.

You Wait for a Bus, Then Two Come at Once

Have you ever heard the saying, 'You wait for a bus and then two come at once'? Well that's what happened next. A red double-decker came careering into the playground, followed by a green double-decker. Only joking. This is what really happened.

Jonno strolled out of the door, smiled at Callum and Jamie and carried on over to where Fifty and I were waiting, both grinning our heads off that he was back. Jamie and Callum didn't seem to take much notice which showed they hadn't realised he was missing. They were still on the hunt for Copper Pie, for definite. And two seconds later, that's who came out of the door – Copper Pie, heading straight for us. As soon as Bee saw him she legged it over. At last, we were all where we should be, on the Tribe patch, with three minutes to go before the bell and a whole bunch of questions.

'Did it go OK?' I asked Jonno.

'Really good,' he said. 'Big Jim is really interesting to talk to. I'd like to go there every day.'

'Did he call you names?' asked Copper Pie.

'No, of course not.' Jonno gave Copper Pie a why-would-he? look.

'And no one saw you?' said Bee.

'No. Actually I had a good idea on my way out. I grabbed a football from a Year 3 and kicked it on to the road so I had an excuse for being there. Then I picked it up and dashed round the corner to the alley. I hid it in a bush at the other end (where the Alley Cats hang out) and did the same on the way back, kicked the ball into the road in case someone was about.'

'We should all do that,' said Bee. 'The ball would be a sort of alibi.'

I knew what she meant, but the ball couldn't actually give evidence to a judge and jury. Although a talking ball defending Tribe would be cool.

'What about you?' said Jonno. 'Did you keep Callum busy?'

'We did,' said Bee. 'But not exactly the way we planned.' She put her hands on her hips and faced Copper Pie. 'So *where* did you disappear to?'

Copper Pie held his hands out as if to say, 'I've done nothing wrong.'

'Come on,' I said. 'We saw you go to the loos, and when you came out we were all going to swap places, but you never came back out.'

'Did you go and check out the gates?' asked Fifty, suspiciously.

'Please don't say you went *outside* the gates looking for Jonno,' said Bee, accusingly. 'Plans are meant to be stuck to.'

Copper Pie sighed. 'I was in the loo, *all right*.'

OK, I got it. He hadn't been anywhere else. He'd been in the loo all the time, doing you-know-what. He wouldn't be any good as a spy or a special agent or whatever if he had to spend ten minutes in the bogs in the middle of a covert operation. I winked at Bee. She got it too. I know because she made a 'yuck' shape with her mouth.

'It doesn't matter,' said Bee. 'What matters is that Jonno helped Big Jim, without getting caught. My turn tomorrow.'

Something about the way Bee said it made me wonder if she was looking forward to bunking off. Weird girl.

Leavers' Week

I was last to the Tribehouse for the Wednesday meeting because Mum was trying out a new recipe and it took longer than she thought. I don't know why she bothered. No one ate much of it, not even her. She says we need to vary our diet. I completely disagree. Varying means adding strangely shaped vegetables in different colours and changing the meat bit into something unrecognisable. The good thing is Mum always gives up with her ideas after a few days and we go back to normal. I said that to Amy, my know-all big sister, and she said Mum feels guilty about spending so much time at work and so every so often she makes a big effort to be a better mum. Flo, my know-all small sister, said she thought Mum would be a better mum if she gave up work and just looked after us. I can't think of anything worse. If she only had us to think about, she'd always be fussing about something. Flo said she'd have more time to make cakes. See, that was all she was really interested in – cakes, not Mum.

'What took you, Keener?' said Fifty. He held out his fist and we all rapped knuckles. It's the fist of friendship. We're meant to start all our meetings with it, but sometimes we forget and sometimes we do it twice. It's a random rule, which is fine, because we make the rules, so we can break the rules. (Except the one that says no one can join Tribe, and no one can leave.)

'I got held up by some evil slurry dished up by my mum.'

Fifty laughed, which was nice. No one usually laughs at anything I say.

'At last! We're all here. Now, do you realise it's school camp next week?' said Bee.

'It can't be,' I said. We had the letter ages ago, but I didn't remember the date we were going. 'No one's said anything.'

'Same,' said Fifty.

'It is,' said Bee. 'It's the week before half-term. I heard the other class talking so I checked on the calendar.'

Another thing for me to worry about, I thought. I won't like the food. I won't like the activities. I don't want to spend all day every day with no escape from Callum and I'll miss my hammock.

Fifty didn't want to go either. He's too small to do all the climbing and survival stuff – the girls manage better than Fifty. And he can't take Probably Rose, his baby sister.

'But what about Big Jim? Who's gonna look after him when we're away?' said Copper Pie. I hadn't thought of that. It was Fifty's turn on Monday and that meant he was going to get away with it because we'd be at camp. *So unfair.* I looked over at Fifty. He was grinning. He'd worked it out too.

'Maybe he'll be much better by Monday,' said Bee.

'Let's decide at the weekend,' said Fifty. 'If he still needs help, maybe we could ask . . . Amy?' Fifty obviously doesn't know my sister that well. She's back together with spotty-face boyfriend so she's too busy snogging to get an old man's lunch.

'Maybe,' I said, because I didn't really want to talk about Big Jim.

'What exactly do we do at camp?' asked Jonno.

'We're in teams and we build bridges and do an assault course and canoe and have a campfire and sleep in a tent,' said Bee. 'Things like that.'

I reckoned she wasn't as keen as she sounded. Bee sleeptalks and sleepwalks which is not ideal on camp – she could end up wandering into a teacher's tent, or Callum's.

'Can Tribe be a team?' said Jonno. 'Or do the teachers pick?'

'We choose. So yes, Team Tribe. But I can't share a tent with you because you're *boys*.'

'Will you go with Lily?' asked Fifty.

'Yes. I rang her and sorted it out.'

'It sounds good,' said Jonno.

'It is,' said Copper Pie. 'No mum. No dad. No brother.' Copper Pie was desperate to go – no washing and an army assault course to play on.

'No dog,' said Bee sadly. (She loves Doodle, but she doesn't love the way her mum babies him, because then he starts thinking he's not a dog but a person and wants to sit on the sofa and eat takeaways.)

'No lessons,' said Fifty.

I didn't say anything. I still had to get through Friday.

'Anyway, we've got work to do,' said Bee. I waited to hear what it was: demand a recycling tent at camp, insist on organic cereal for brekkers . . . but it was a complete change of subject.

'You know Jonno and Lily are going to be on the Leavers' Week Committee?' I nodded. 'Well we're going to come up with some ideas so that it's not the same old stuff.'

'What is the same old stuff?' said Jonno.

We always forget he only came to our school this term. He's so part of Tribe that it feels like he's been here as long as us.

'Do you want the bad stuff or the good stuff first?' said Fifty.

Jonno pushed his glasses up his nose so he could actually

see through them rather than over them. 'The bad.'

So Fifty filled in the details of the last week of term, our last week of being juniors before we all go up to secondary school. The week that's meant to be a 'Celebration of Our Time at the School' – gross.

'OK. There's a leavers' assembly on the last afternoon and we all get given a certificate that says something good about us, like, *He always opened doors for people* or *She was a good citizen*. All the girls cry, I don't know why. There's a disco.' (No way was I going to a *disco*.) 'And the girls stand one side and the boys stand the other and the idiots dance in the middle. And the girls wear make-up and look awful.'

'How do you know that?' said Jonno.

'Year 5s get to go too,' said Bee. 'But only me and Fifty went last year.' She paused and looked at Fifty. 'Why did we go?'

'I think my mum made me go and you said you'd come with me.'

'I'm nice, aren't I?' said Bee.

Everyone shook their heads.

'Anyway,' said Fifty. 'Worst of all, there's a yearbook. We have to give in a photo and write something cheesy to go underneath, and everyone gets a copy. It's pure puke. People write stupid things like, *Thank you so much to all my classmates. I'll miss you so much. Hattie. Kiss Kiss.*' He made kissing noises to make the point. I cringed. I mean, who wants a picture of Callum to take home and treasure? I'd rather just have a Tribe yearbook.

'Is that the end of the bad things?' Jonno asked. Bee answered before Fifty could. She never lets anyone talk for very long without interrupting.

'Yep, that's about it, unless the committee comes up with some more tortuous ideas, like a prom night with girls in ridiculous dresses and boys in suits, which they won't because *you* won't let them.' She gave Jonno the stare. He nodded like one of those dogs people have in the back of their cars.

'So, on to the good stuff,' said Fifty. 'We get two film afternoons. They make the hall like a cinema and we get to have popcorn.' He grinned to show that a cinema afternoon was definitely the top event of the week. 'We get to vote for which films, and there are always two because the girls and boys can never agree.'

Silence.

'Is that it, then?' Jonno was obviously expecting more. 'Is that the end of the good things?'

We all looked at each other. And then we all said, 'Yes' within a nanosecond of each other.

'Right. Looks like we need to come up with some way of having some fun in Leavers' Week.' Jonno looked around. 'Any ideas?'

Too right there were, but as usual they were mostly rubbish, and a few were lunatic.

IDEAS FOR LEAVERS' WEEK

- An eating competition – if you're sick you're knocked out
- A graffiti competition – first one to be caught gets to clean it all up
- A show, Year 6s mimic the teachers and the rest of school guess who's who
- The whole week off school
- A sponsored silence – for the teachers
- Wearing jeans to school, and free cakes for afternoon break
- Bring your pets in
- Take over the staffroom at lunch and make the staff play in the playground
- Year 6 run the school for the week
- A bonfire (Fifty's idea of course)
- Recycle everything school uses for a week, so they keep on doing it (Bee's)

'Can we forget about Leavers' Week for a bit? It's not for ages,' said Fifty.

'But this is our chance to make sure we have the best time, and maybe even change what happens after we leave,' said Bee. 'Jonno's meeting the other class reps on Friday lunchtime.'

'But it's only Wednesday,' I said. 'Why don't we all think about it on our own? Someone will think of something good by Friday.'

'Same,' said Fifty.

Everyone agreed, so we stopped making plans and did what we usually do – talked about random stuff, laughed about all the amazing things Tribe's done, watched Fifty and Copper Pie play fight, and ate some biscuits left over from the last meeting (they weren't very nice – that's why they were left over) and some raisins Fifty had brought with him.

There were still two days till my turn to go to Big Jim's. I did the ostrich thing – head in the sand.

Bee's Turn

I woke up on Thursday – only one more day till my turn. Time to think of ways to get out of it, I decided. I may be a Triber but that doesn't mean I'm stupid. And bunking off is stupid. I moved from my bed to my hammock – swaying is good for thinking.

> ## WAYS TO GET OUT OF VISITING BIG JIM
>
> 1. Be off sick.
> • Except with a mum who's a doctor it's difficult to fake illness.
> 2. Get Big Jim to say he doesn't need any help.
> • Ideal but impossible.

3. Tell *my mum*, or Fifty's, all about it.

• But Tribe wouldn't forgive me if Big Jim got carried off to a home and left there forever. (And what about Carlotta the cat?)

4. Invent a dentist's appointment at lunchtime so I wouldn't have to creep out. I could forge a letter from Mum, if I dared. Or Fifty could do it for me.

• Best idea so far. Although means I'd still have to do the bunking off.

5. Swap with Fifty.

• Except Fifty would have to be stupid to agree as he won't be doing it.

6. Faint at lunchtime and get sent to the school nurse.

• This idea rocks.

By the time I'd bolted my breakfast I felt much better. Anyone can pretend to faint. The Tribers might suspect I was putting it on, but I could cope with that. Last mouthful – I scraped the bowl a couple of times with my spoon to annoy Amy – and then I headed off to meet Fifty.

We talked about Probably Rose (which means he talks and I agree). I know better than to have an opinion of my own about her. I once said she'd hate him when she was older and I reckon it nearly broke our friendship. Although Fifty goes on and on I can listen and think at the same time, so it's not that boring. I just say 'Yes' or 'No' or 'Umm'.

'Probably Rose ate all her Weetabix.'

'Umm.'

'Do you think Probably Rose will be in top set for maths? She can count raisins already.'

'Yes.'

'Mum says Probably Rose is going to start doing full days at nursery. I bet she'll be home-sick. What if she wants to come home but they don't understand what she's saying?'

I scrolled through my normal answers: yes, no, umm. None of these were right. So I said, 'I expect the nursery is used to dealing with babies that can't speak properly.' Oops! I could tell from Fifty's face I'd said the wrong thing.

'But she can speak properly for her age, can't she, Keener?'

It's safer when I stick to yes, no, umm. 'Yes,' I said.

As usual, the others were there before us. Jonno was studying the tree stump on our patch. He keeps an eye on all his insect friends. They love rotting wood. Bee and Copper Pie were doing nothing.

'We've been waiting for you.' Ah! Not doing nothing – waiting for us.

'Why's that?' said Fifty.

Because we're friends, I thought. *Duh!*

'Because there's a problem,' said Copper Pie.

My danger sensors weren't working at all. I was blissfully unaware that my life was about to fall apart. I was thinking: broken mobile phone, homework left at home, Copper Pie's brother's got the flu, Doodle has diarrhoea . . .

What I wasn't thinking was . . .

'Bee's cracked her tooth. Her mum's made an emergency appointment at the dentist. It's 12.30 today. That means she can't help Big Jim at lunch. So it's your turn, Keener. You're bunking off today. Bee'll do it tomorrow.' Jonno's voice sounded very grown-up and serious, like the announcement made by Neville Chamberlain in 1939 that the British were at war.

> 'I am speaking to you from the cabinet room at 10 Downing Street. This morning the British ambassador in Berlin handed the German government a final note stating that unless we heard from them by 11 o'clock that they were prepared at once to withdraw their troops from Poland, a state of war would exist between us. I have to tell you now that no such undertaking has been received, and that consequently this country is at war with Germany.'

Miss Walsh played the recording in class. It's scary. And scared was exactly how I felt. I thought back to my 'Ways to avoid having to visit Big Jim'. The dentist excuse was obviously out of the question – Miss Walsh would never believe we both had sudden toothache – so I had to faint. And to make sure the other Tribers didn't suspect I was faking when I collapsed at lunch break, I had to convince them that I was prepared to bunk off (even though I wasn't).

'OK,' I said. 'Me, today. Bee, tomorrow. That's fine.' Fifty gave me a funny look, so I added, 'Gets it over with, anyway,' to make me seem reluctant but resigned to it. I had to put on a good show. Fifty knows me too well.

'Good on you, Keener. Copper Pie said you'd bottle it,' said Bee.

Oh great! That's all I needed.

'No way,' I said, trying to look determined. The bell went and I made a quick escape. The less interrogation, the better. The more time to think things through, the better.

Keener
Bunks Off

The morning disappeared. One minute I was in the queue to go into school for morning registration. Then I was handed a kit list for camp next week. And the next thing I knew, Bee'd gone off to the dentist and I was in the lunch queue – the Tribers had let me in at the front so that I could scoff and go. I wonder if I can explain how I felt. I wasn't in a panic, like when you're nervous and there are things jumping around in your tummy, it was more like I'd been anaesthetised ready for an operation. I was numb.

'Jacket potato, please,' I said to the dinner lady. It didn't even sound like my voice.

At the table I could hear my friends talking, but it was like the words had been put through a scrambler because I couldn't understand what they were saying.

'Don't forget to grab a football, like I did.' Jonno's voice came through the fog.

I nodded. But I wasn't going to take a football, was I? No, because I wasn't leaving the school grounds or helping Jim, I was going to faint. Some time soon.

'Get going, Keener,' said Copper Pie. I looked down at my plate. It was empty apart from a few pieces of potato. They looked a bit like snowflakes. I like snow. Sledging is fun, but what I really like is building. I made an igloo last winter. A real one, with snow bricks that I shaped using the garden spade. It stayed frozen for ages after the rest of the snow had disappeared. *Disappear . . . that's what I needed to do*. I got up.

'We'll keep an eye on Callum and Jamie,' said Fifty.

'Good luck,' said Jonno.

'Same,' said Fifty. Even though I was about to go, I could tell from Fifty's face that he didn't believe I was really going through with it. (He was right, but he didn't know it yet.) I smiled a plastic smile, and left.

Where shall I faint? Where shall I faint? I walked towards the entrance hall. Loads of people pass through, including teachers. It seemed a good enough place. I decided to hold my breath. When I was smaller I used to do that a lot (whenever things didn't go my way, according to Amy) and faint without meaning to. I took a huge breath in.

And would you believe it? Nothing happened. Except eventually I had to breathe out. I must have looked a bit odd, just standing there. I wished I'd had acting classes so I knew how to go floppy. There was the noise of people coming down the stairs. *Just do it,* I thought. So I did. I closed my eyes, bent my knees and wobbled. I was about to let myself drop to the ground when someone poked me in the back.

'What are you doing, Keener?'

It was Flo. Why does my little sister always turn up when she's absolutely totally *not* wanted?

'I'm . . . waiting.'

'Waiting for what?'

'Waiting for Fifty.'

'He's gone in the playground. I saw him.'

'Thanks, Flo.'

There was nothing else for it. I walked towards the door, darted out, grabbed a football, kicked it over the school railings, ran after it, picked it up and then kept on running, with my heart drumming away inside. All the way to Big Jim's.

Beans
on Toast

I ran in through the gate and banged on the back door.

'In you come,' said Big Jim's big voice.

'So it's you today, is it Geeker?'

'I'm Keener, not Geeker.'

'Keener, Geeker, I don't know. "Swot" you'd have been called in my day, or "Encyclopaedia-on-legs".' He laughed.

I laughed too, not because it was that funny, but because I'd made it to Jim's. I had, for the first time in my life, and hopefully the last, left school without permission, also known as truanting or bunking off. It felt quite good.

'What do you want me to do?' I asked.

'If you don't mind, I'd like a nice cup of coffee and if you could make me a sandwich, that'll be grand.'

'No problem.'

I filled the kettle and switched it on. Then I went to get a mug off the shelf and realised they were all in the sink. In fact the sink was piled high.

'Shall I wash up quickly?'

'That'd be a fine thing. Thank you, Keener.'

While I washed up the stuck-on food and the gooey treacle in the bottom of the mugs, Big Jim talked to me about his school days. He left school when he was fourteen and worked in a solicitor's office. He used to steal the stamps and sell them half price. He worked in lots of places and then joined the army. I don't know how old he is but he said he was in the Second World War. Awesome.

I got the bread out. It was a bit hard.

'Would you rather have toast? I could heat up some beans?'

'Go ahead. I was never much of a sandwich man but I decided not to let old Robin Redhead near the gas.' He chuckled. 'What a boy, he is!'

I poured the water on the coffee and added the milk (there wasn't much left), stirred the beans and buttered the toast. Big Jim carried on chatting.

'I had a friend like that Copper Top when I was young. Football mad. No time for books or learning. We raised hell at school. Always up to something, bit like those Tribers.' He winked at me.

I put everything on a tray and carried it over to him. He rested it on his lap and I sat on the other chair.

'How are you?' I asked. Mum always gets us to say that if we ring our aunts or uncles to say thank you for our birthday presents. She says it's important to show an interest in other people.

'Not so bad. The wrist's a bit of a nuisance. Weak as a kitten. But I'm not so sore as I was.' He shifted in his seat a bit and held his side. I guessed that was where his ribs were bust.

I didn't know what to say next – I wouldn't be much good as a nurse – so I asked about the cat.

'She'll be along later. Ginger Nut fed her this morning so it'll be teatime before she comes sniffing.'

When he said 'time' I sprang up. I looked at my watch. 'What time is it?' You know if you're really frantic you can't speak properly or work out what someone else is saying, well I couldn't tell the time. I could see the clock face and the hands but they didn't make sense.

'Nearly half-past one,' said Big Jim. 'You'd better be off.' I already was.

'Thank you, lad,' I heard as I ran out of the door, up the side of the house and *SMACK* straight into Copper Pie's mum carrying a black bin liner out to the wheelie bin.

NOOOOO!

For Once Shouty Shouty Doesn't Shout

We call Copper Pie's mum Shouty Shouty, because she shouts. (You probably could have worked that out for yourselves.)

'Keener, what are you doing here?'

There was a pause so large that it couldn't really be called a pause.

'I...'

And another one, about the same size.

'We...'

'Come with me.' I did what she said. People generally do. I was too late to get back to school before the bell anyway. My whole life was over. I'd be expelled. I'd have to go to school somewhere else. I'd be a new boy, like Jonno was, except no one would make friends with me, because

I'm a geek. And the geeks wouldn't make friends with me because I'd been expelled, so they'd think I was trouble. Mum would be mad. Dad would be *disappointed*. The Tribers would forget all about me and let someone else join like Ed or Lily. One day one of them, probably Fifty, would say, 'Do you remember that blond kid we used to know? He didn't like runny food. And he could remember the number plates on everyone's cars.' And the others would all shake their heads, shrug, and carry on being Tribers without me.

TRIBE WITHOUT KEENER

- No one would be able to add up
- No one's dad would take Tribe out for a day's surfing
- The safe wouldn't be in the Tribehouse (it's Keener's)
- No one would write anything down (no Fact Files)
- No rules (Keener is the rule monitor)
- There wouldn't be any wimps in it (that's really mean – who said that?)

I followed Copper Pie's mum into the kitchen. She pointed at the chair so I sat in it, while she said something to one of the girls that works for her in the nursery.

'Come on then, Keener. You know you're going to have to tell me so we may as well get on with it.'

She was right. So I did. I didn't look at her, I looked at my knees. But I told her all about Big Jim, and Copper Pie's promise to look after him, and how we agreed to share the job so there was less chance of getting caught by Callum. I waited for the yelling to start, but it didn't. So I risked a glance at her face.

Now, I know I've known her all my life, but I don't think I'd ever looked at her properly before. She's actually got quite a kind face and is even sort of pretty-ish. (Don't ever tell anyone I said that.)

'Well, first things first. We need to call the school and tell them you're not under a bus. I'd run you in but I can't leave the nursery until Brooke gets back from her lunch break. I don't suppose your mum's around?'

It was Thursday. She does a late surgery. I shook my head.

'Well, you can help me for a bit. And don't worry, Keener. You meant well.'

It was astonishing. She was being really understanding. She gave me some carrots to peel and chop, and went off to ring the school. When she got back I was dying to ask her what had happened: *Had she spoken to the Head or just Miss Walsh? Did they know I was missing already or had word not spread yet? Had the Tribers told Miss Walsh I'd bunked off because they thought I might be under a bus and wanted her to ring round the hospitals?*

I did the cucumber next, and then put the cherry tomatoes in a bowl. I was filling the water jug when Brooke came back. I knew it was Brooke because Copper Pie's mum said, 'Hello Brooke'. Then she said, 'Can you hold the fort for me while I run Keener back to school? I shouldn't be long.'

'Of course,' said Brooke. She hung her coat on the pegs by the door, put on a red apron and took over from me. 'Bye,' she said as I left. 'And good chopping – my carrots are never that tidy.'

'Bye.'

Isn't it funny how you can bunk off and everyone treats you really nicely? Or should I say, everyone *so far.*

'Jump in,' said Copper Pie's mum. If you actually jumped into a car, you'd hit your head. I stepped in. 'The Head's expecting us, Keener. I want you to tell the truth, the way you told me.'

I wanted to do what she said because she'd been so nice, but knew I couldn't. I'd be ratting on Copper Pie and Jonno if I told the truth, because they'd bunked off too. But maybe I could say I was the first to go round to Jim's, then they'd be in the clear.

'But then —' I said.

Copper Pie's mum interrupted me. 'I know what you're going to say. But you must tell the truth, even if it means getting your friends in trouble. Even if it means getting my son in trouble. Do you understand?'

I did. Stupid, stupid me! If only I hadn't done the

washing-up, or bothered with the beans on toast, I'd have been back in plenty of time. By not hurrying, I'd dropped everyone else in it. What was I thinking? I'd acted as though I'd dropped round for afternoon tea, when I should have been like a German in the Second World War racing to do just enough to keep the Jewish friend in the attic safe and well, *without* getting caught by the Nazis.

We walked in and went straight to the Head's office, a place I've seen too much of lately. It was pretty full already. There was Miss Walsh, the four Tribers, Marco, Ed and Lily. *What was going on?* The Tribers looked a bit confused too. They were probably wondering what I was doing arriving back at school with Copper Pie's mum. Copper Pie's face was more than confused. He looked terrified, which was understandable. *Your mum and the Head in a room together – not ideal.*

'Keener! You're all right.' What exactly was Bee expecting? Me on a stretcher? Me, but with some vital bits missing?

I nodded. I was fine. It was her who didn't look right.

'Are you all right?'

She pointed at her lop-sided mouth. It looked like she'd had a stroke. (Did you see the FAST ads on the telly? I remembered it all just in case.)

> ## IS IT A STROKE?
>
> Face - is it drooping on one side?
> Arms - can the person raise both their arms?
> Speech - is it slurred?
> Time - to call 999

'Dentist,' she said, in a lispy, saliva-y voice, complete with dribble. That explained it.

'Hello,' said Copper Pie's mum. 'Here he is.' She pushed me in front of her.

'So, we find ourselves here again, Keener. How much time do you think the Tribers have spent in this room over the summer term?'

There isn't an answer to a question like that.

'The answer is too much,' said the Head.

Or maybe there is.

Bee butted in. 'But we were only trying —'

'Thank you, Bee. I've already heard your version of the story. And as much as it is commendable to want to help someone in need, leaving school without permission is not the way to do it.'

Bee shut up.

I could understand why the Tribers had been dragged up to see the Head. I mean, we were all in it together, and Bee had obviously filled in the details (which was good because it meant I didn't have to), but why were Ed and Lily and Marco there too?

'Keener, you have caused quite a commotion this afternoon. You are fortunate in that so many people seem to be concerned about your welfare, and that they had the common sense to report your absence.' I couldn't bear the not knowing any more. I interrupted.

'What are they all doing here?'

60

'We're making sure you're not minced under the wheels of a pick-up,' said Ed.

'We were worried,' added Lily. 'When you weren't there at afternoon registration Bee whispered to me about the bunking off. I told Ed and he told Marco. When Miss Walsh went off to find out if you were with the nurse, we decided we had to tell someone.' She looked across at Ed. 'The Tribers were trying to think of a way to find you without admitting the truth but . . .'

Her voice trailed off.

'You did the right thing coming to me, Lily,' said the Head. 'And you Ed, and you Marco.'

That cleared things up. I never realised I was so popular. The only thing left to clear up was the punishment.

'Right, you've all seen that Keener is safe and well so, Miss Walsh, could you please escort your pupils back to the class and salvage what remains of the afternoon's lessons.' We must have all looked a bit surprised to be let off so easily, but she hadn't finished. 'I shall consider what action to take when I have spoken to the parents concerned. Thank you.'

The Head turned to look at Copper Pie's mum. 'Perhaps we could have a word now?'

'Of course, but I'm afraid it will have to be quick as I left the nursery short-handed.'

'Let's get on, then. Goodbye children.'

We left the Head with Shouty Shouty (who needs a new nickname, like Nicey Nicey).

The Lull
Before the Storm

I trailed after the others, and shut the door. The punishment was obviously going to come later. We just had to wait it out. I didn't know how I felt, but however I felt, at least I knew we were all in it together. If I'd had to pretend I was the only truant I'd have felt a whole lot worse, that's for sure.

'What happened, Keener?' I ignored Fifty's whisper. Walking along behind a frosty-looking Miss Walsh wasn't the best time to talk about how I got caught bunking off. He said it again, only louder.

'Fifty, I'm sure he'll tell you all about it later, and hopefully he might add how sorry he is to have caused all this fuss. As the Head said, we've wasted quite enough of the afternoon already.' Miss Walsh wasn't in a good mood. 'And in future, not even the very tip of a toenail of a member of 6W will scrape outside the school gates in school hours. Understood?' I had a picture in my head of us all dressed in Egyptian clothes, wearing brown leather sandals with long yellow toenails scraping the ground in front of us. And that thought reminded me of something else.

THE WORLD RECORD FOR THE LONGEST FINGERNAILS

(That should be renamed the world record for the most revolting thing ever.)

Shridhar Chillah, from India, grew the nails on his left hand for fifty years. They were brown and knotty-looking, like tree roots, and they twisted and curled. If I touched one, I'd have to wash my hands ten times in super-biological germ powder and never eat anything with my hands ever again. They weighed so much that his hand was damaged and eventually he had to have the nails cut off. He did it to be famous, but he ended up deaf in his left ear from the strain it put on that side, and he couldn't use his hand any more. That's totally stupid. And a complete waste of his life.

An equally mad American lady grew the nails on both her hands. They also looked hideous, but at least they were clean.

> If I was going to get a world record I'd choose one that didn't ruin my life, like eating the most cream crackers or spending the most time in a hammock.

I sat in class, listening to Miss Walsh going on. No one did anything wrong, which made a change. Alice kept her hand down. Jamie kept his mouth shut. I think everyone knew Miss Walsh was ready to blow. It probably wasn't that great to be the teacher of the class that was always in trouble.

Eventually, after the longest lesson ever, it was time for afternoon break. We rushed to the patch, them desperate to hear what had happened to me, me desperate to find out what they thought was going to happen to us, Copper Pie desperate to know what it all had to do with his mum.

The conversation went like this:

Copper Pie: How come you came back with my mum?

Bee: Did she catch you at Jim's?

Jonno: We were really, really worried.

Fifty: Thought you'd been run over. You know, flattened.

Bee: We didn't want to tell.

Jonno: There wasn't any other way. Ed and Lily were right.

Fifty: I thought you were dead. Squashed. Like a hedgehog.

Bee: But not as prickly.

Jonno: And better at surfing.

Copper Pie: How come you came back with my mum? (My turn at last.)

Keener: I ran straight into your mum when I left Big Jim's. She was putting the bin out.

Copper Pie: No way! She never leaves the house in the day. Never. (He kicked the tree as he said that.) So unlucky!

Bee: Did she shout at you?

Copper Pie: Of course she did. That's all she does.

Keener: No. She didn't shout. She was nice. She let me make the snacks for the nursery kids.

Copper Pie: Are we talking about my mum here? (I nodded.)

Jonno: Why didn't she bring you back right away?

Fifty: Same. Then we wouldn't have had to imagine you flat, complete with tyre marks.

Keener: She couldn't leave until one of the other nursery people got back from lunch. I didn't exactly mind. I wasn't in a hurry to find out what was going to happen to me.

Fifty: What *is* going to happen?

(A long silence. Too long to be called a pause. They seemed to be happening a lot.)

Copper Pie: I'll get shouted at by Mum, and she'll ban me from the telly or something else I like. And the Head'll make me sit outside her room again, probably till Leavers' Week. (He looked glum.)

Keener: My mum won't believe it. And when she realises

I really did bunk off, she'll . . . I don't know what she'll do. I've never been in the sort of trouble your mum gets to hear about. (I looked glum.)

Jonno: I think my mum and dad might be OK about it. I mean, it depends how you look at it. If you look at it through Big Jim's eyes, we did the right thing.

Fifty: Do you think they'll tell *our* mums? (He was talking to Bee. They were the only two that hadn't bunked off.)

Bee: The Head said 'the parents concerned'. That might mean ours too, I'm not sure. But we might have to tell them anyway. (Fifty's face didn't seem to agree.)

Fifty: Why?

Bee: Well, we've got to stop bunking off. So the problem that started all this is still there – Big Jim. If we can't help him, we've got to find someone who can, before they call the hospital police, or whoever's waiting to take him away.

Keener: He's not our problem any more. Not now Copper Pie's mum knows.

(Copper Pie made an I've-just-realised-something-important face. That's a rare thing.)

Copper Pie: I reckon that's why she didn't shout at you, Keener. She feels *guilty*. (He smiled.) Maybe I won't get banned after all. Maybe I'll get thanked!

Bee: Mums are one thing we'll just have to deal with. I'm not worried about that, I'm worried about school. The Head won't leave it, she'll be cooking up some way to make us suffer.

At exactly that moment the Head's head appeared out of the door. The Head's head scanned the playground and settled on us. The Head's head focused, by narrowing its eyes, and then zoomed in.

'In my office after school, please. The five of you.'

The Head's head zoomed out, turned about, and disappeared.

'Let's not go,' said Copper Pie.

'Same. Let's catch a bus and then a train and then a taxi and then a ferry . . .' said Fifty.

I knew he was joking. That sentence is out of a picture book Fifty used to keep in his desk when we were in the infants. It was about a boy going to stay with his grandad for the very first time. Fifty liked the pictures. (I quite liked them too but I pretended to like the digger book the other boys were mad about.)

Bee was thinking, I think. She had her mouth shut anyway. Finally she said, 'Let's go and say that unless the Head helps us look after Jim, we'll keep bunking off.'

'You are a lunatic,' I said. 'Firstly, that's blackmail. Secondly, the Head can't look after a stranger just because he happens to live next door to someone in one of her Year 6 classes – she has to look after the school. Big Jim is not her job.'

'It's not anyone's job. That's the point. So unless someone makes it their job, Big Jim will probably die.' Bee can be a drama queen.

67

We joined the line to troop back into school. Flo was at the back of her queue and as she went past she said, 'Keener, Jack said you bunked off. I said you'd never bunk off because you're a scaredy-cat.'

I looked at my sickly little sister with her yellow hair and pink lips (she was wearing Amy's lip balm with a rosy tint again – strictly not allowed).

'So I bunked off. Who cares?'

If I'd had a camera on my phone I'd have had the best picture ever. Her bottom lip fell so far away from her top one that I could see all the lumps where the bottom of her teeth were stuck into her jaw.

'I'm telling Mum.'

What did it matter? She'd know soon enough.

The Storm

We all stood in a line opposite the Head, who was sitting at her desk. She said, 'I have a problem on my hands.' Copper Pie looked down at her hands. *What an idiot!* 'You are, as I've said before, not irresponsible children, in the main. Yet you insist on repeatedly flouting the rules. And this time, you have pushed me too far. To leave the school without permission not only puts you in danger, but shows the school to be failing in its duty of care to your parents to look after your safety whilst you are in its care. Do you understand?'

Of course we did. We're not in Reception. I nodded.

'Yes,' said Bee.

'But my problem is not how to deal with this affair, as much as how to let the rest of the *school* know that this behaviour will not be tolerated, for I understand word has got around that the "Tribers" have been leaving school in the day. This may be seen as a reason to look up to you, to want to be like you.' *The other kids want to be like me!* What a great thought. Trying to stop myself grinning made the corners of my mouth hurt, so I gave in and grinned behind my hand. 'I cannot have you seen as heroes by the younger and more impressionable children in this school. So, I need you to help me show the rest of the school that breaking the rules is never the answer, even if breaking the rules helps someone else.'

'Excuse me,' said Bee, 'but how are we going to do that?'

'I was coming to that, Bee. Every spare minute you have tomorrow will be spent sitting outside my office. That means before school – if you are here before the bell, morning break, lunch break and afternoon break. This will allow plenty of time for the other children to see what happens to those who are not good citizens of the school, and it will also allow me to keep an eye on your whereabouts. And Jonno, in the circumstances, I don't think we will need you on the Leavers' Week Committee after all.'

Hardly an imaginative punishment. But at least we weren't suspended and Leavers' Week is rubbish anyway. Trust the Head to bring up the 'citizenship' thing. It's her latest fad. I looked around at the rest of the Tribers to see if they thought the same.

Oh no! I could see Bee was getting ready to blurt

something out. Her lips were pressed tightly together as though they were trying to block the words that her brain was trying to push out. They came out anyway. 'I don't see that what we did means we *aren't* good citizens. I think it means we *are* good citizens. We helped someone who needed help. That's kind.'

Shut up, Bee! Why does she always have to say what she thinks is right. Why can't she just pretend to agree out loud and disagree inside? That's what I do.

Bee didn't shut up. She carried on. 'Citizenship means getting on with everyone, being kind, helping out, stuff like that.'

'And it also means respect for yourself, your fellow pupils, your teachers and the rules of the school. You should *not* have broken the rule about leaving school grounds, and I will not have you answer me back, Beatrice.' The Head was livid. Her face was bluey-red and the veins in her forehead were bulging out, like snakes crawling down out of her hair Medusa-style. I was quite frightened. I didn't want the Head to be my enemy, Tribe's enemy.

We left her office, me first.

Jonno said 'Thank you' as he left. Wish I'd thought of that.

'One more thing.' The Head's voice stopped us all dead. 'Be very clear, this is not a school that will allow its reputation to be damaged by a group of children who think they know best. This is not a school that will allow truancy.

And if you think being a Tribe gives you the right to do as you please, then be warned, there will be no Tribe at this school.'

It was just like Neville Chamberlain's speech all over again. The Head was threatening to declare herself at war with Tribe.

Reputations at Stake

I walked out of school to find my mum and Flo waiting, which was odd because usually they go home in the car and I walk home with my friends. Actually, it was even odder than that, because it was Thursday, which is Mum's late night at the surgery so it should have been Amy picking Flo up, not Mum at all. But in a way none of it was odd, because my mum had obviously found out that her hard-working, honest boy was in fact a truant, and that explained her change of plans. (I was so angry about the Head saying Tribe was damaging the reputation of the school that for a minute I'd forgotten about my own reputation.)

'I've had a call from the Head. I think you'd better come in the car with me, don't you?' Mum said.

Fifty, Copper Pie, Bee and Jonno all melted away, leaving me on my own.

I nodded. 'Yes, Mum.'

Flo started to ask questions but for once Mum shut her up. 'Flo, this is something that your brother and I need to sort out on our own, thank you.'

Flo made an ugly face. I preferred it to her normal one. It suited her personality.

At home we had a snack (cheese scones and apple juice) that we ate in complete silence. I had trouble swallowing the scone so I washed small pieces of it down with gulps of juice to stop it getting stuck. Eating when you're nervous is a dangerous activity.

'Flo, can you go and watch CBBC while I have a chat with your brother?' I wanted to go with my sister. I wanted to be little again and for *Clifford the Big Red Dog* to be my favourite programme.

Flo walked ever so slowly towards the living room, looked back and smirked at me. Mum saw, and shut the door on her, leaving the two of us. I am so rarely in trouble (although it happens much more now I'm a Triber than it ever did before), that I didn't know what to do with my face, or my hands, or whether to stand up or stay sitting where I was. Mum sat down next to me, so that sorted out one question.

'I think you'd better tell me all about it.' Mum put her hands on the table, pressed together like she was praying. I did the same with mine. It wasn't that comfortable but I thought it made me look sorry. Mum looked sorry and she hadn't even done anything.

I took a deep breath and started at the beginning and finished at the end. I didn't leave anything out, not even the bit where I tried to faint. I reckoned the more Mum knew about how much I didn't want to do it, the quicker she'd forgive me.

'I'm so sorry, darling.' Mum put her hand on top of mine. Weird. I didn't think the forgiving bit would come before the telling-off bit. I waited to see what was coming next. 'I feel dreadful that you didn't feel you could come to me or Dad. Surely you know we would always try to help someone?'

No, I thought, but I said, 'I thought you'd have to tell someone.' That was a lie. I never thought seriously about telling Mum at all. What could she have done? Given up her job as a doctor to look after Copper Pie's neighbour? I *don't* think so.

'It doesn't matter now. What matters is that you're safe.' Mum's eyes were watery. 'But you must promise to come and talk to me if there is ever a problem again that you need help solving.' A tear trickled down Mum's face. 'Promise?'

I nodded. She wiped her cheek.

'Although it was wrong to leave school without permission, going to help Jim was *very, very* kind. I think your Tribe should feel proud.'

Mum being so nice was quite odd. I was half waiting for a telling-off but half getting the idea there wasn't one coming.

'The Head said she would leave the disciplining to the parents. All she intends to do is ask you to sit outside her office tomorrow.'

I nodded again. And because I hadn't spoken for a while I added, 'Can I go now?'

'Of course, you can. I'll call you when tea's ready.' I got up. 'And don't you worry about Jim. I'm going to make a few calls.'

Finally, I escaped up to my room.

Big Jim's a Wow
at the Red House

Copper Pie sent me a text: *BIG JIMS WORKING AT RED HOUSE*.

That's what his mum's nursery is called, The Red House. Although it isn't actually red, it's brick-coloured.

I texted back: *WOT?*

So he rang me. My ringtone is *Mission: Impossible*. Amy says it's lame. Hers is a recording of herself saying, 'Pick up. Pick up'. It's freaky, her voice without her body.

'Keener, it's me. You'll never guess.'

'Don't tell me,' I said. 'Big Jim's working in the nursery.'

'How did you guess?'

'You texted me, idiot.'

'Oh yeah.' He didn't say anything else. He's not that good on the phone.

'Are you going to explain, then?'

'Mum said she felt guilty. Guilty that I didn't think she'd help, and guilty that Big Jim thought she'd turn him in. So, I'm in the clear and Big Jim's coming in here every day till he's better. He's gonna eat with the kids. Mum went and fetched him after she left the Head's and by the time I got in he was sitting in the armchair and all the little brats were sitting round his feet. They loved him.'

I could just see it. Big Jim with his wild white hair and his shirts with big checks that Bee says are like tea towels, laughing his big laugh. Even if he wasn't ace at making up fantastic stories just the look of him would make you smile, because *he* smiles all the time, and teases, and laughs, and he's huge. (I should have said that earlier – it explains his nickname.) He's taller than a normal door, and probably almost as wide.

'So problem's solved.' I was pretty pleased. I'd bunked off and managed to stay out of trouble even though I was caught. Amazing.

'Yep. And Mum's let me choose tea. We're having pasty and chips, and then me and Dad are going over the park with a football. See ya.' He ended the call before I could reply.

I looked around my room, deciding what to do before tea. *Pack*, I thought. I knew it was three days till camp but it wouldn't hurt to start sorting out what I wanted to take. I got out my rucksack, the one that I take on holidays, which is bigger than my school one. And that was when my phone rang again, and it was Bee, and I didn't like what she had to say.

'Keener, the Head's just rung my mum.' *So what*, I thought. The Head had spoken to all our mums. But I said, 'Has she?' to sound interested.

'She told Mum that she'd decided it would be better for us to use next week's camp to "reconnect with the other members of our year group".'

'What does that mean?'

'It means, she's going to split us up. We'll all have to be in separate groups. It'll be awful. I could be with Callum . . .' She paused.

Even worse, I could be with Callum, I thought.

'Why did she say that?' I said. 'That's not what she told us in her office.'

'She must have changed her mind.'

A thought came to me – *if Bee hadn't disagreed with the Head about 'citizenship' the Head wouldn't have devised an extra punishment*, but I kept it hidden because Bee wouldn't have liked it one bit. *Her big mouth could do with staying shut sometimes.* I kept that thought hidden too.

'I'm going to ring the rest. We need a plan. I'm not spending a week in a group with Alice, or Callum or Jamie. No way. Bye.'

Bee rang off before I could reply. I sat holding the phone for a bit wondering what sort of plan could change the

Head's mind. The answer was as clear as if it was written across the blue sky in white smoke from a Boeing 747.

N   O   N   E

I don't know how long I stayed like that. Completely still. But eventually Mum called us for tea and on the third shout I did what she said and went downstairs. I wasn't looking forward to the school trip anyway. Now it was fifty times worse, knowing I wouldn't be with mates.

Mum and Amy and Flo chatted about rubbish: Flo's latest pom-pom animal (a mouse), Amy's spotty boyfriend and Mum's asthma clinic (my sisters like hearing all about Mum's work – no idea why).

'What's up?' Mum was looking at me. It wasn't surprising really. While she'd been chatting and eating, I'd managed to sit at the table and not eat even one pea, or one grain of rice, or one flake of salmon (in honey and soy sauce which is quite nice).

'Camp,' I said.

'It's fun,' said Amy. 'You have a fire and the teachers mess about, and there's loads of cool stuff to do.'

'It's only fun if you're with your friends,' I said.

'What do you mean?' said Mum. 'All your friends will be there.'

'But we won't be together,' I said. 'The Head said she won't let us be a team at camp next week.'

'Because you skived off school?' Mum asked.

I nodded. Mum obviously didn't know anything about it. She said 'Did she now?' in an odd voice, and made a face that I couldn't quite work out. Amy started telling us all about her week at camp. I stopped listening.

There were still a few days to go. I decided to push all the worry out of my brain for a while. (I did it the usual way – making up stupid words that don't exist, like *compodasty* and *mewminny*.) It helped – I ate my tea and even managed to forget about camp for a bit. I reckoned when the Tribers were all together, one of us would come up with an idea. One of us always does.

KEENER'S DICTIONARY

compodasty (adj.) – completely deadly and nasty

mewminny (noun) – small cat noise

nipallot (verb) – to tickle someone who's not ticklish

roobic (noun) – biscuit made from kangaroo

optastic (adj.) – describing the best view ever

fungnail (noun) – toe cheese

reddimling (verb) – trying to make your face less red

After tea I helped Mum in the garden. She's a hopeless gardener – her fingers aren't green, they're toxic. We made the rockery together. I did all the hard work lugging the stones. She did the planting. It's all weeds now. We attacked them together but Mum got fed up after a bit so I finished it myself. I had a super-deep hot bath after that, fell into bed and went straight to sleep without letting anything to do with camp sneak into my thoughts.

All I Can Think About Is Camp . . .

Fridays should be good. Dad always has a Friday feeling – that means a good feeling, because it's nearly the weekend. My Friday started off bad. From the minute I woke up (*thanks for the early morning body slam, Flo*) all I could think about was being away from home for four days and having to team up with kids I don't like and, worse, sleep in a tent with kids I hardly know. I tried the *compodasty* stuff but my brain wasn't playing. My brain was only interested in what I was going to do about CAMP.

There was only one way I was going to feel better. I had to get to school, and quick. I needed the Tribers. I wolfed a couple of wet Weetabix (they don't require chewing, they don't taste of anything either), shouted 'Bye' to no one in particular and headed off. I texted Fifty on the way to make sure I didn't have to spend ten minutes waiting for him at the corner where we meet.

'What's the hurry? Flo bullying you again?'

Ha ha, Fifty! I ignored his stupid remark and launched straight in to the CAMP problem. Fifty listened to me go on about how bad it was going to be, and when I stopped so he could say something back he said, 'Same'.

It's no help having a friend like Fifty when there's trouble. We didn't need 'Same'. We needed solutions. We needed the others.

As we turned out of the alley I could see Copper Pie standing by the school gates, eating a bag of crisps – from a distance they looked like salt and vinegar. He usually has beef.

We were about to cross the road when I heard a dog bark – it was Doodle, dragging Bee and Jonno, and way behind was Bee's mum. Thanks to Doodle's speed we all got to the gates at the same time (except for Bee's mum).

'What are you stuffing those for?' said Bee to Copper Pie. Doodle tried to put his nose into C.P.'s pocket. He could obviously smell the remains of his endless snacks.

'Ran out of beef,' he said, between chewing. His teeth were covered in a layer of mashed crisps.

'Idiot, I meant why are you eating crisps for breakfast? They're one of the top five bad foods. It's so unhealthy,' said Bee. Her mum had just caught up with us – she shrugged her shoulders as if to say, 'I don't know where she gets it from.'

'It's not breakfast. That was ages ago.'

Bee rolled her eyes, like a mum whose child won't eat his greens.

'Are we going in?' she said. It did seem a bit odd standing at the gates and not going through them.

'Do you think we're meant to go straight to the office or are we allowed in the playground before registration?' asked Jonno.

I knew the answer but I wasn't going to say it. If no one else remembered, I wasn't going to be the one making us sit like lemons (but not as yellow) outside the office before school.

'Office,' said Fifty. 'The Head said every spare minute.'

Jonno gave Doodle a big rub on the back, and kissed his neck. That boy is weird. And we left Bee's mum and walked slowly towards the main door.

I don't know about the rest of them but I couldn't have cared less about the uncomfortable seats waiting for us. I was worried about being under canvas with Callum, or jammed up next to Jamie in a sleeping bag.

Copper Pie opened the door. Fifty went next, then Bee. I was next. As I put my foot on the step I heard Flo's foghorn voice.

'There's Keener, Mummy. He's going to sit by the Head's room, isn't he, Mummy?'

I carried on in, without a glance. The five of us walked in complete silence along the corridor. There were only three chairs outside, but still no one spoke. Jonno and Copper Pie went and got two chairs out of Mr Dukes' classroom. They lined them up and we all sat down . . . and waited for the bell, or the Head – whichever came first.

But what came first was a whole lot more amazing . . .

Mum's
Army

There was the sound of lots of feet, some clompy and some clickety. We all zoomed in on the direction of the approaching army. It didn't sound like kids, and teachers don't usually go round in herds.

Incredibly, it turned out to be mums. To be specific, my mum, Bee's mum (but no Doodle), Copper Pie's mum (she was in the front) and Fifty's mum. I strained to see behind, in case Jonno's mum was there too, but there were only four. I don't know why I said 'only' – I mean four mums coming into school on a Friday morning was quite a few.

'What's going on, Mum?' said Bee.

Copper Pie's mum was obviously the Commanding Officer. She did the talking.

'We've come to sort out the Year 6 camp. It's your last

trip in this school. Don't you worry. You'll either be together, or you won't be going.'

I wanted to cheer. My face was flooding with bright pinkness. It was like having Jiminy Cricket or a fairy godmother or a genie or something come and grant you a wish like in fairy tales. I looked over at Mum and she winked. I wanted to give her a great big hug. I couldn't remember her ever standing up for me before. I had a look round to see what the other Tribers thought of it all.

Copper Pie was holding his fist in the air, 'Yes!'

Bee had pushed her fringe out of her eyes and was standing up, hands on hips, like a scary Amazon.

Fifty was still sitting, grinning a grin so big it was like the Cheshire Cat's grin in *Alice in Wonderland* when the rest of the cat has disappeared.

But Jonno . . . well, he was . . . sitting, looking at his knees.

I nudged him. 'We've got an army of mums to fight for us. Tribe wins again.'

He raised his mop of bushy hair to look at me. 'Great. Really great.'

I got it. I expect Bee got it before I did – she's good at people. I bet Fifty got it too – he's like his mum, he knows what's going on underneath. I bet Copper Pie still hadn't got it, but he would, as soon as it was pointed out. Jonno was the only one of us whose mum hadn't come to the rescue. Jonno's was the only mum who didn't care. It's funny, I liked her when I first met her. She wears beads in her hair that play tunes as she walks, and she's really . . . sophisticated, like in a magazine at the dentist's. But I don't think she's that nice because we never get invited to his house (I've been twice, once invited, once not) and she didn't come to the summer fair, and she made Copper Pie turn the telly off the only time he ever went there. The more I thought about it there was quite a lot of evidence against her.

Copper Pie's mum knocked on the Head's door, three times.

'Come in,' said the voice.

I wish I could have seen the Head's face, but there wasn't a chance. The four mums marched in and the door banged shut.

We did a totally spontaneous silent Tribe handshake. It was hard not to laugh. Whoever would have thought the mums would come into school to stick up for us? It was almost too fantastic.

The bell went.

'What do we do?' said Fifty.

We all wanted to stay to see what happened but we knew that would only cause more trouble.

'Let's go,' said Bee. 'Come on, Jonno.' She grabbed his arm and said something I couldn't hear. I expect she was trying to make him feel better. I think Copper Pie must have heard because he punched Jonno – that means 'You're our mate, even if your mum's let us down.'

* * *

The day went on and on and on. We sat outside the Head's office at morning break, at lunch and at afternoon break. The Head didn't say one word to us. Not one word. We all wanted to ask her what had happened, but no one dared. Judging by her face, she detested us even more than she had the day before. Good job we were only a month away from leaving junior school. I texted Mum but she didn't reply, and neither did Fifty's mum. Copper Pie didn't dare text his mum and Bee said her mum had left her phone at Bee's brothers' place. It was no good, we had to wait until we got home. Loads of the little kids who saw us sitting in a line in the corridor giggled and pointed and all that, but it didn't matter. What mattered was that we had to be allowed to be Tribe at camp. That's what mattered.

We agreed to all go home together, and although the Tribehouse would have been good, we agreed to go to mine because Fifty thought his mum was taking Probably Rose to have her hair cut. (What hair? The little wisp on top? I didn't have my hair cut until I was about three. Probably Rose isn't even two. My mum took me to the barber and he got out his electric razor thing and I was frightened so I kicked him. That's quite unlike me – I must have been terrified.)

So we legged it to mine, and we arrived seconds behind Mum who had parked the car and was just helping Flo get her 'absolutely amazing' (code for rubbish) painting out of the boot.

'Hello,' said Mum. 'Do we have the pleasure of the whole Tribe?'

We all nodded. I knew I had to be the one to ask – it was my mum – but I was having trouble getting the words out. *What if it hadn't worked? What if the Head had told our mums to go away and leave the running of the school to her? What if she'd said Tribe was expelled and we could only continue in school if we were Tribe-less? What if...*

Mum saved me.

'I expect you'd like a blow-by-blow account of our meeting with the Head.'

'Yes, please,' said Bee.

The Blow-By-Blow Account

'The Head didn't look too pleased to see us,' said Mum. 'But we explained that we felt strongly that you shouldn't be punished so severely for trying to help Jim.'

'But they shouldn't have left school, Mummy,' said Flo.

Mum gave Flo the evil eye. *Go Mum!*

'You can either stay in here,' said Mum. She paused and put her finger in front of her lips. 'And listen. Or you can go in the living room.'

Flo made the ugly face. Mum ignored it and looked at Fifty. 'Your mother was excellent, Fifty. She was most concerned that if you weren't allowed to be with your friends at camp as a direct result of helping someone, the lesson you would learn would be to not help someone another time.'

What an awesome argument. The Head was teaching us

how *not* to be good citizens.

'What did she say to that?' I asked, dying to hear that she'd collapsed sobbing and begged our mums to forgive her.

'I think that was when there was a knock at the door and Jonno's dad came in. I didn't catch his name, is it Andrew?'

All of a sudden Jonno was smiling big time.

'Yes. No, I mean, it's Adrian. What was my dad doing there?'

'The same as the rest of us,' said Mum. 'Looking after our Tribers.'

Copper Pie punched Jonno. I think he was a bit overenthusiastic because Jonno lost his smile for a second and rubbed his arm.

'Go on,' said Bee, adding, 'please' at the end.

'Well, there's a man with a genius for talking! Adrian was most charming, and after thanking the Head for helping Jonno to settle in, and thanking all of us for having such welcoming children,' (she smiled at us, one at a time) 'and apologising for being late, he turned our rather confrontational beginning into the most agreeable meeting. The Head agreed she had been a little hasty in her decision about camp. And Adrian suggested she was in fact showing how very concerned she was for the safety of her pupils, who should *not* be out roaming the streets.'

'So are we in the clear?' asked Fifty.

'Absolutely,' said Mum.

It was time to celebrate. Jim was going to get to stay at

home, thanks to Copper Pie's mum, and we were going to be together at camp. Mum brought out some chocolate chip cookies and made up a jug of blackcurrant. We all sat down at the table, except Jonno.

'I think I'll get off, if that's OK?'

'Don't be stupid,' said Fifty. 'This is chocolate.' He pointed at the plate of cookies, that was already half empty.

Jonno wobbled his head from side to side as though he was a set of scales weighing it all up. 'No, I'll get off. I kind of want to thank my dad.'

'Thank your dad later,' said Copper Pie, taking two more cookies to go with the one still in his mouth.

'Let him go,' said Fifty. 'Leaves more for us.' He was joking, almost certainly.

I didn't say anything, and it wasn't because I had my mouth full of sweet crumbly chocolate, it was because I understood. Tribers are meant to stick together, but that doesn't mean they have to stay in the same room. Jonno wanted to go, and that was fine. Wherever we all are, we're still a team. We're still Tribe.

'Hang on a sec, Jonno,' said Bee. 'Tribe handshake.' She slapped down her hand and the rest of us followed.

One, two, three. We threw our hands high in the sky.

I had a Friday feeling. A really good one. I reckoned we all did.

Under Canvas

All Packed Up

By Sunday night I was all packed up. One sleeping bag with small pillow inside, one middle-sized rucksack with all my clothes for the week including a waterproof and my wetsuit, a towel and a wash bag, one pair of wellies hung on the outside, one small rucksack for days out, everything named. Mum had given me a pep talk that covered subjects ranging from sleep problems to advice about food.

MUM'S PEP TALK

Homesickness
Lots of children feel this. It's OK to feel homesick. It may happen at night. It will pass. (This has to be the most unuseful advice ever.)

Temperature

In the day it can vary enormously so wear layers
e.g. a short-sleeved T-shirt, a long-sleeved T-shirt
and a sweatshirt. Take off or put on as necessary.
(Thank you, Mum. I could have worked that out.)
At night, if cold, wear socks and a woolly hat.
(They're called beanies, Mum.)
The water will be cold. (Really?) Wear your wetsuit,
even if other children don't. They may not own one.
(I will not be wearing a wetsuit if everyone else is in
trunks. I'd rather freeze to death in my trunks.)

Clothes

Everything is labelled, except pants. Don't bother
reclaiming lost pants found under the groundsheet
– it's embarrassing. (Too right.)

Safety

Listen to the instructor carefully. All the activities
are safe as long as you abide by the rules. (This is
Keener, Mum. I'm a rules person. I will only disobey if
absolutely necessary, and agreed with the Tribers.)

Hygiene

Please wash, Keener. (I am the boy that doesn't like
sticky things on my hands. Of course I will wash.
Copper Pie may not.)

Food

Wash your hands. (See above.) Choose dishes cooked for a long time, like stews, to avoid tummy upsets. (It's not a restaurant.)

Bowels

Drink plenty of water to help you go to the toilet. A change of diet can make you bunged up. (I'm embarrassed now, Mum.)

Everything about me was ready, except me. I didn't want to go. I'm just not the sort of kid that wants to go away for a week with school. I like holidays, but that's different because you're with your family. I sat on the bed and tried to give myself a Keener pep talk. It went like this: *Keener, you'll be with Tribe all week, eating, sleeping, mucking about. It'll be good.*

I repeated it a few times and I could feel my brain starting to believe it might be true, and then Dad came in. His pep talk was quite different from Mum's, no toilet or bathroom tips.

DAD'S PEP TALK

I know you're probably feeling like you don't want to go, but, believe me, other children will be sitting at home feeling just like you do. You will all have a good time when you get there. You might not enjoy every minute, and sometimes you might want to come home, but most of the time you'll be busy having fun.

Remember, it's only four days and three nights, and then you'll be home again. You're lucky – you've got four fantastic friends to keep you company. Not everyone has such close mates to rely on. So if you're feeling a bit sad, go and find a Triber. In no time at all you'll be back home, sitting right here on this bed, full of stories about how Tribe had a great time at camp.

I decided to focus on Dad's last sentence. Being back home again.

Flo woke me up by dangling two of her homemade pom-pom animals over my face. It took me a few minutes to work out that I wasn't in a woolly animal dream and that it was setting-off-for-camp day. I had a poke around inside my head to decide how I felt – not too bad. In fact, I was quite keen to get on with it. The sooner we got there, the sooner I got back home.

The Bus

I didn't walk because I had too much stuff. Mum dropped me off. She kissed me (in the car, not in front of the world) and said 'You'll be fine.' And then she drove off.

The whole of Year 6 had been told to stand in the netball court next to our bags. Some Year 6s did exactly that. A whole other lot of Year 6s ran around like lunatics, excited about the trip, I guess. And there were a few waiting with their parents.

The Tribers stood together. I didn't feel much like talking so I let them chatter on while I inspected everyone's luggage.

Jonno had a proper walker's rucksack with a tiny sleeping bag strapped on the front. All very organised.

Copper Pie had a Man United sports bag with big

black wellies sticking out of the pocket, a bright red sleeping bag in a see-through plastic bag and a small day sack, bursting full. I didn't need to ask – he'd obviously brought snacks.

Bee's rucksack looked brand new. It had a surf-type pattern on it. I quite liked it. She was wearing her wellies.

'Where's your sleeping bag?' I asked.

She turned to answer me. 'Crammed it inside,' and then went back to the conversation which seemed to be about whether Doodle would go back to being a badly behaved puppy without Bee there to make her mum treat him like a dog, and not a baby, for four days.

Fifty's luggage was totally un-camp-like. He had one of those wheelie suitcases that businessmen take on aeroplanes (and business women, Bee would say). His sleeping bag was tied on to the handle of the suitcase and so were his wellies. On his back he had one of those cool rucksacks with water in them that you can suck as you go along (I think they're called CamelBaks, that would make sense wouldn't it? You know, humps).

'Is that new?' I pointed at the tube, resting on Fifty's shoulder.

'Yes. Mum bought it. Doesn't want me to get dehydrated.' He did a great big suck. 'I like it. It's like a dummy.'

'What's nice about a dummy?' I said.

'Don't know, I never had one. Neither does Probably

Rose, but she sucks her thumb so I bet she'd like one.'

Dummies were obviously more interesting than Doodle's behaviour. Everyone piled in.

'I had a dummy,' said Copper Pie.

'That figures,' said Bee. We all laughed. He looked confused.

'She means you are a dummy,' said Fifty.

'They're not called dummies any more,' said Jonno. 'They're pacifiers.'

'That's a good idea,' said Fifty. 'Giving them a name no baby could possibly say.' He demonstrated. 'Give me my gaga gaga pac-if-i-er, gaga.'

'It's because dummy isn't a nice name,' said Bee.

'What about plastic people in shop windows?' said Fifty. 'They're dummies.'

'And we do dummies in football,' said Copper Pie. 'You pretend to do something but you don't.'

'And they have dummy runs and that means practice runs,' said Jonno.

'But if you're a dummy it means you're stupid. So that's why they changed it. You can't call babies stupid. End of.'

The bell went. The dummy conversation, even though it was boring, had done a good job of passing the time.

Miss Walsh stood by the gate and said something in a loud voice. I didn't get what she said because I was too busy staring at how funny she looked. Starting at the bottom, she had on big boots and those plastic things that go up to your knees to stop your trousers getting wet (hers were green) and baggy trousers and a belt with all sorts of things hanging off it (like a cowboy, but no guns) and a waterproof with reflecting stripes and a whistle round her neck and, worst of all, a brown leather hat with a big brim, like Australians wear – although they have corks hanging off theirs. She looked like we were going on an expedition, not getting a bus to Devon.

'Class 6W, line up in twos, please.'

I took a step forwards to be next to Fifty. Copper Pie took a step backwards to be next to Bee. Jonno stood on his own. That's the trouble with five, it doesn't go into pairs. Luckily Marco was near us and so he filled in the gap. Ed and Lily were behind. We started to troop on to the bus. We had to put our bags in a pile, all except for the day sacks. That took ages. Loads of bags weren't done up properly, wellies kept appearing from nowhere, some kids tried to take their bags on board and got sent back to the pile, Alice wanted to sit at the front in case she was sick so she caused a blockage at the front of the bus. We were at the back of the queue, with only Callum and Jamie behind us.

'Hey, Fifty, have you packed your suit and tie?' shouted Callum. He'd spotted the executive luggage. We ignored him. But he was obviously bored, and wanted to annoy us.

'Fifty, have you packed a ladder? No way will you get

over the wall on the assault course without one.' Jamie and Callum started laughing. I looked at Fifty. He looked a bit white. I thought I should say something, defend my friend, but my mind was a blank computer screen.

Bee leant forwards. 'Ignore him, Fifty.'

'Have you packed a compass, Callum?' said Jonno. 'We wouldn't want to lose such a helpful member of the class.'

Jonno does it again! The friendly voice as though he's being nice. Callum never knows what to say back.

The queue in front of us gradually disappeared up the steps of the bus and it was our turn. We dumped our stuff in the pile and just as I was about to step on the bus Callum and Jamie pushed in front. They grabbed a double seat. There didn't seem to be any more. *Great! We'll have to split up*, I thought. I scanned the seats again for a Tribe-size gap. There wasn't one. Fifty found a seat by Roddy, and there was one in front of him by a girl in the other class, so I sat down there without looking at her, or at Callum, who I'm sure was enjoying the fact that Tribe was scattered all over the bus. Bee sat diagonally opposite me, but poor Jonno had to sit by Miss Walsh and Copper Pie was left with Alice. We were going to have to get our act together. There was no point making camp worse by being separated. We needed to be at the front of the queues, ready at all times. It was the first camp rule. I decided to think of a few more on the way to wherever we were going.

I only remember getting to 8 – I must have fallen asleep.

TRIBERS' CAMP RULES

1. Be prepared (stolen from the Scouts).
2. Avoid the team Callum's in.
3. Help each other. (I was thinking of Fifty and the wall on the assault course.)
4. Beat Callum's team at everything.
5. Be the advance party to bagsy the best (food, seats, whatever) for Tribe.
6. Share snacks (Copper Pie probably had nice biscuits in his day sack).
7. Keep the Tribers' secrets (I was pretty sure C.P. would have Trumpet* in his bag).
8. Stick together.

* Copper Pie's cuddly elephant

I always do that on journeys. In Reception I fell asleep on the way back from the museum and everyone laughed at me because I was sucking my thumb. After that I started sitting on my right hand (the side I sucked) on trips to stop it happening again. I don't have to worry about that any more because I gave up thumb sucking when the dentist said if I didn't stop I'd need braces to fill the thumb-shape gap. Braces mean pain and I don't do pain. Full stop.

I wiped my chin. (Why do you dribble when you sleep sitting up?)

'Where are we?' I turned round and asked Fifty.

'Nearly there,' he said. 'We just passed a sign that said *Highwoods Activity Centre, 4 miles.*'

I looked out of the window, which meant I had to look at the girl next to me.

'Hello,' she said.

That's all I needed, a friendly girl. My face went pink so I quickly looked over towards Bee in case the girl noticed.

'Your face is all red, Keener.' *Thanks, Bee.* 'Are you hot?'

'Bit,' I said. I looked down and tried to use willpower to make my face skin colour. Willpower takes a while, the next time I looked up it was because there were shouts of 'We're here.'

The bus turned up by a big green sign into a leafy drive that looked like it went on forever. I thought the driver was going a bit fast but he'd obviously passed his driving test or he wouldn't be a driver so I tried not to worry about all the lurching. There was one final turn where everyone on my side had to hold on to stop being catapulted over to the other side of the bus and then the brakes were slammed on and we were all thrown forwards and then tossed back again. I hoped we'd have a different driver on the way home.

Mr Morris got up and gave us instructions about getting off – usual stuff like no pushing. I was going to wait till there was a gap but then I remembered the camp rules about being prepared and I elbowed my way into the line of kids in the aisle. Callum was trying to do the same but I got ahead of him.

I grabbed my rucksack from the pile the driver was chucking out of the boot – it was near the top – and followed Miss Walsh's ridiculous hat towards the tents. We'd already agreed the groups we were in for sleeping but I wanted to make sure nothing went wrong. She stopped at the end of the path to give out more instructions to the ones in front, which included me.

'All the tents are the same, but they're numbered so we know who's where. When your group has assembled, one of you has to fill in the card inside with your names and bring it to the mess tent.'

'What's the mess tent?' asked Alice, who had somehow got in front of Copper Pie even though she was by the window and he was in the middle.

'Think of it as headquarters. It's for meetings, some mealtimes, and if there's a storm or any other emergency, it can be accommodation.' Miss Walsh pointed at a massive tent in the middle of the field.

As the only Triber in the lead group I decided to bagsy the best tent. *Start as we mean to go on,* I thought. Only trouble was, I didn't know which position was best – near the mess tent, or not near the mess tent? But then the answer dawned on me, near the loos was probably best, in case we had to go in the night . . . but hang on, wouldn't it be smelly?

Callum ran past me and shot into tent number 7. That was the clue I needed – I headed for the one furthest away from Callum, number 3. And then I remembered Bee wasn't allowed with us because she's a girl and I bagsied number 2 as well, by standing between 3 and 2 until she arrived.

'Who are you with, again?' I asked her.

'Lily.'

'And?'

'And no one. It was meant to be Rose and Molly but they're both off sick. Lily says that Molly didn't want to come and Rose was too scared to come without Molly.'

'Lily can speak for herself,' said Lily's voice very loudly and right by my ear. 'And she thinks they didn't come because they didn't want to be in a tent with Bee.' Bee stuck her tongue out at Lily and then they both started laughing.

'A tent to ourselves. We're *so* lucky.' Bee grabbed Lily's arm and they disappeared inside.

Where were the other Tribers? I wondered. I took the card and started to fill in our names, looking up every so often. There were loads of kids wandering about, but none of my friends.

Mr Morris was coming towards me but I assumed he was going to veer off to wherever he was going before he walked straight into me. But he didn't.

'Keener, your friends are in what's called the "san".' He could see I didn't know what the *san* was. 'The health centre, Keener. They said you'd be concerned, so I've come delivering messages.'

He looked at me. I didn't know what he wanted me to

do. Go. Stay. Tell Bee. I decided on 'Tell Bee'.

'I'll tell Bee.'

'Good, that was my next job. And if you want to see them, they're over there, behind the shower block.' He pointed in the general direction of the brick buildings.

I got Bee and we ran. How bad was it? Who was it? I was pretty sure it would be Fifty. I mean, he is the smallest. I was worried. Very worried.

Sick in
the Sink

It wasn't Fifty, it was Jonno, and he wasn't well. He looked awful. He was sitting on the bed in the 'san' and his pale face looked even paler than normal and he looked smaller than normal and even his afro looked less bouncy.

'What's wrong?' I asked.

'He's car sick,' said Fifty.

'Bus sick,' said Copper Pie.

Jonno leapt up, shoved his head in the sink and made the most disgusting retching noises.

A lady I'd never seen before (glasses, short dark hair) came in. I supposed she was the nurse or something.

'He's no better then?'

Fifty shook his head.

She sighed. 'I doubt very much that this is travel

sickness. I think this boy will have to be sent home. We can't have tummy bugs at camp.'

Jonno lifted his head out of the sink. 'I promise, it's travel sickness. I always get it on coaches,' he pleaded.

'Now then, there's no need to get worked up. It's not your fault and I'm sure you're very disappointed —'

Jonno looked like he was about to interrupt but instead he started retching again.

'I'll come back in a few minutes,' the lady said.

As soon as she was out of the door we all started talking at once (except Jonno, of course).

'She can't send him home.' (Me.)

'It's so unfair.' (Bee.)

'She's probably in league with the Head.' (Fifty.)

'Yeah, determined to split up Tribe.' (Bee.)

'Can't you stop puking, Jonno?' (That was Copper Pie.)

'No, he can't, idiot.' (That was Bee.)

'But he needs to, and double quick.' (Fifty again.)

'Are you really coach sick, Jonno?' (Me.)

Jonno nodded into the sink.

'He says he always gets sick when he gets off,' said Fifty.

'I don't think there's a cure for travel sickness,' I said. I should know. My mum's the doctor. That shut everyone up. I could feel a sick feeling growing in my stomach too — we couldn't have camp without Jonno. It would be like having . . . a full English without the bacon.

CAMP WITHOUT JONNO
WOULD BE LIKE:

- A Spitfire without any bombs
- A party without cake
- A day without lunchtime
- A Cornish pasty without the meat
- A telly without a remote
- Surfing with no surf wax
- Christmas with no Christmas tree
- Easter with no Easter eggs
- A fire without Fifty

'Actually, there might be a cure . . .' Fifty pulled a little white plastic bottle with a yellow label out of the pocket of his joggers.

'What's that?' I asked.

'One of Mum's magic potions. She gave it to me in case I felt stressed.'

Copper Pie snorted. He thinks Fifty's mum is weird. (She's not, but she does have kooky ideas. For example, she says if you make a picture of what you want to happen in your mind, it's more likely to happen for real. So if you see yourself winning the lottery, you're more likely to get the six balls. Mad, clearly. She also uses flower remedies – they're like medicines but made from flowers. She gave Mum some to help her give birth to Flo. Mum pretended they'd worked but really she thinks it's all a pile of nonsense.)

'Stressed about what?' asked Bee.

Fifty looked down at his feet. (He has extremely small trainers. Makes sense – he has extremely small feet.) 'You know, about the wall and all the other "challenges" that are more of a challenge if you're half the size of everyone else.' He twisted the lid off the bottle and used the dropper to drop some of the stuff into his mouth.

We all stared as though something dramatic was going to happen, like Fifty was about to grow a moustache or sprout wings or horns. But nothing did. Except that Jonno stood up, wiped his face on a piece of paper towel and said, in a weak un-Jonno voice, 'Bung it here. I'll try anything. I don't want to go home.'

Fifty handed him the bottle. 'Four drops should do it.'

Jonno let out a big sigh and then droppered the squashed flower arrangement into his mouth. He swallowed. We stared. He kept his lips pressed tightly together. We all carried on staring. There were still no horns, wings or beards.

'It helps if you believe in it,' said Fifty.

Jonno opened his mouth. 'I believe in it.'

Bee giggled. It did sound a bit strange, like Jonno was pledging his soul to some witch doctor.

Footsteps.

'She's coming back,' said Bee. 'Come on, Jonno. Last chance. No more retching.'

He nodded. I crossed my fingers behind my back. There

was no point, I knew that, but I was so desperate for Jonno to be better. We couldn't lose a Triber on the first day. Jonno took a couple of breaths, and as she walked in he said, 'Thanks for looking after me. I feel much better now. Can I go?'

She gave him a suspicious look, over the top of her glasses. He smiled. He was still totally white and a bit floppy but at least he didn't have his head in the sink.

'I'm not sure,' she said.

'Pleeeaaase,' said Bee. 'He's fine, really.'

The nurse had a good look at him, as though he was a puppy she was thinking of buying. *It could go either way*, I thought.

Fifty did an exaggerated yawn, as though we were all boring him, and then stepped in front of the nurse and came out with a load of make-believe.

'He'll probably be in the middle of an important meeting, so he won't be very pleased, but if you call Jonno's dad he'll tell you that Jonno is *always* sick when he gets off a bus. He's fine on the journey, but every time he sets foot on terra firma,' he paused for an eye-roll, 'he vomits. You're lucky he made the sink. On the trip to London he did it all over the steps of the Natural History Museum. Ask anyone, Jonno's a puker.' Fifty took out his phone. The screen said *Jonno Dad*.

The nurse hesitated. *I* knew Fifty was faking, but *she* didn't. Fifty didn't even *know* Jonno's dad's number, we'd *never* been on a bus with Jonno before, and he definitely hadn't *ever* been sick on any steps of any museum anywhere near us. *Would it work?*

'That won't be necessary. I can see he's a much better colour now. Jonno, may I suggest you make sure staff are aware of your tendency to feel unwell to avoid such a situation in future. Mr Morris was clearly ignorant of your condition.'

'Absolutely,' said Jonno, in a loud clear voice. 'Thank you very much.'

We made for the door, to find Mr Morris coming through it.

'How's the patient?' he said.

'Fine, thank you,' said Jonno, who was looking much better. *Go flower potion!*

I led them to the tent. Fifty's suitcase wheels didn't like the grass so he had to carry it which slowed us down a bit, but we managed to dump all the stuff before the camp horn sounded which meant it was time to assemble outside the mess tent. I just had time to congratulate Fifty on his quick thinking (typing *Jonno Dad* into his phone was a brave move – if the nurse had tried to call it the game would have been up) before we were told to 'settle down and listen'.

We all sat on a huge plastic sheet. It was the usual safety-respect-rules-good-citizens-representing-the-school type of talk. The interesting bit was the plan for the day. Lunch, then a tour, then duck racing, then chores, supper, quiz, bed. It didn't sound too bad.

I Love
my Sleeping Bag

Seriously, my sleeping bag felt like the best bed in the world. Camp was tiring. Fifty tried to talk to me but I couldn't be bothered to answer. Someone was already asleep – I could hear some little piggy snorts. Copper Pie, I reckoned. He had Trumpet at the bottom of his sleeping bag so no one could see it. Question: If no one could see it, how did I know? Answer: Because that's what Copper Pie always does.

We'd had a good day. The place was basically a field, a few buildings, a river, a big wood (that we only saw from a distance), the assault course (that weaved over the river and back again) and the best bit, the beach. After the tour was over it was time to get into groups – no worries. Tribe stood together. But then the nurse with the short hair and glasses, who obviously wasn't a nurse at all, announced we needed to be in sixes because there were forty-eight of us in total, not fifty, and that meant eight groups of six, not ten groups of five. Lily was the obvious choice to join us but she was already with Ed and Marco. Callum and Jamie were in a two. *Don't put one of them with us*, I thought. For a minute it looked like disaster but thankfully Lily started organising everyone and somehow she ended up with us, and Marco and Ed ended up with quite a cool group and Callum and Jamie were put with four kids from the other class. Naming our team was easy. Although Lily insisted it be called 'Tribe + Lily' because she's not a Triber.

TEAM NAMES
(mostly rubbish):

- Tribe + Lily (us)
- Mountainboarders (Marco, Ed and others)
- Missiles (Callum, Jamie etc.)
- We Hate Spiders (girl I sat next to on the bus and giggly friends)
- Axemen
- Flower Power (Alice's lot)
- Hogwarts (so lame)
- Team GB

It was time for duck racing. We had such fun. There were heats and then a semi-final and a final to find the winning team. Between us we set the whole course up. We made a finishing line using sticks as poles to hold the string that ran across the river. The start line was the bridge. Every team had to make something to catch the ducks with so that they didn't go all the way to the sea. (We criss-crossed some string over the end of a forked stick.)

It sounds a stupid kind of race, but the river was flowing really fast and the ducks (they were rubber, not real – that would be cruel and Bee would have had to go to the san because she's frightened of flappy birds) went really fast too. There were rocks and weeds and stuff that got in the way, so one minute the Tribe duck was in the lead and the next it was last, and then it would find a nippy bit of current again and overtake.

We ran alongside the river shouting – everyone did. Our duck was green. In the practice run it came last, but after that we got better and better. It was all to do with the angle between your duck's beak and the flow of the river, and the speed of launch (or it could have been luck). We made it to the semis, beat Callum's lot (even though they'd called themselves Missiles!), and then it was time for the final – Tribe versus Mountainboarders (Marco, Ed, etc.). It was absolutely brilliant. One of the camp instructors (not the nurse, a man called Max) got everyone to vote for who was going to win, and our supporters stood one side of the river and theirs stood on the other. It was Jonno's turn to let go of our duck (with the beak pointing just off-centre, slightly to the right) and Marco launched theirs. What a race! Everyone was screaming. We were winning. They were winning. We got stuck. They got stuck. Our duck found a way through a tangle of weeds and was storming ahead when their duck found some engine boosters somehow and shot straight down the middle of the river to win by about three duck lengths. We didn't mind, well I didn't, but what happened next was hilarious. Marco was so excited he jumped into the river to fetch his duck and held it up in the air shouting something in Portuguese (the water came up to around his middle) and everyone started clapping, even Max, who you'd have thought should have been dragging him out.

Some teams helped with tea – it was stew and we had it in the canteen – and then we all sat on the groundsheet again for the quiz. Mr Morris was the quizmaster. He was funny – he kept using different accents and giving us hints that weren't hints. Miss Walsh was in charge of scoring. Every round was about something different and at the end of it each team took up their sheet for marking. We were OK on history (thank you Fifty for paying attention in class), good on sport (well done Copper Pie for paying attention to the Premier League), and music (Lily's speciality), OK on geography (Jonno and Bee) and literature (me, and it means books), but hopeless at entertainment (loads of questions about film stars), and brilliant at science and nature (Jonno got the lot).

At the end there was a joke-telling contest while they added up the scores. Fifty stood up and reeled off about twenty jokes one after the other like he was a stand-up comedian so no one else got a look in. He was awesome. There were prizes for the top three teams. We scraped second, one point ahead of the team with the friendly girl from the bus in it (called We Hate Spiders), but then we went way ahead when Max awarded three bonus points for Fifty's one-man show. Our prize was a box of Maltesers, which we ate outside tents 2 and 3. Then Bee and Lily disappeared into their tent and I went to the shower block to do my teeth. I'm pretty sure Copper Pie didn't bother to do his. I didn't care. All I wanted was to have the longest sleep ever. I turned over in my sleeping bag. I thought I heard a beep, like something being turned on or off, but that was the last thing I remember so maybe it was me being turned off for the night.

Wakey Wakey

Mr Morris poked his head into our tent and said, 'Wakey wakey.' It was a horrible shock – being fast asleep and then a second later being face to face with a teacher.

'Where's Fifty?' he said.

The answer was pretty obvious – in his sleeping bag. I looked across. *Ah! Perhaps it wasn't so obvious.* Fifty had either wriggled down to the bottom, or gone for an early morning jog. I kicked his bag to see which was true.

'Get off me,' said a muffled voice.

'Fifty,' said Mr Morris again.

A head of black curly hair crept out of the opening. Followed by an eye.

'Yes, Mr Morris.'

'I gather you have brought a mobile phone with you,

spotted by a member of the activity centre staff when you visited Jonno in the san.'

Fifty nodded.

'Hand it over. You can have it back on Thursday, when we hand you back to your parents. You know the rule.' The rule is no phones allowed – it's meant to stop people ringing their mums begging to go home.

Fifty disappeared down into his sleeping bag and came up with his phone. Mr Morris retreated out of the flap.

'You brought your phone,' I said. That's called 'stating the obvious'.

'You know I did. I pretended to have Jonno's dad's number, didn't I?'

Me, Jonno and Copper Pie all went 'Oh yeah' at the same time.

There was silence and then Copper Pie said, 'Why'd you do that?'

And Fifty said, 'Same reason you bought Trumpet,' and threw himself at Copper Pie's sleeping bag. He tried to burrow in and find C.P.'s elephant. Me and Jonno sat up in our bags and enjoyed the show.

I had no idea what a phone had to do with a cuddly elephant but the wrestling was good fun.

Eventually Copper Pie gave in and fished Trumpet out himself.

'There. All right, so I brought him. What are you gonna do?'

Trumpet looked a lot older than the last time I saw him properly (which was probably in Reception). His trunk was hanging by a thin bit of grey string.

Fifty shrugged.

'Actually, I brought something in case I was homesick too,' said Jonno. (That's when it clicked – Trumpet and the phone were both homesickness cures. The mysterious bedtime beeping was Fifty checking in.)

'What?' we all said. We were getting good at speaking at the same time, like a chorus or backing vocals.

Jonno put his hand inside his pillowcase and pulled out a bullet-shaped piece of stone. Odd thing to choose. He turned it round, looking at it from different angles.

'It's my favourite fossil.'

I made a mmmmm noise, which was the best I could muster. It was a stone, that's all.

'Where did you buy it?' asked Fifty.

'I didn't buy it,' said Jonno. 'I found it, on my first fossil-hunting trip with my grandad. I've got better fossils, you know, ammonites, crinoids, but this belemnite was the first really good one.'

'Cool,' said Copper Pie, shoving Trumpet out of sight again.

'What have you got, Keener? Cuddly toy? Bit of your old baby blanket?' asked Fifty. I didn't like the way he said 'baby'.

'Nothing,' I said. And it was true. I may have been the

one dreading coming to camp but I hadn't brought anything, unless they counted keeping Dad's last sentence in my head, telling me I'd be back home soon. So much for me being the wimp. I smiled at the three of them to make sure they realised that, for once, it wasn't *me* who was the baby.

Max told us the day's activities while we ate breakfast. (The nurse stood by his side and added extra details.) It was all wasted on me. I couldn't hear a thing because Copper Pie was cramming so much food into his mouth at once that he kept having to do a sucking-up slurp to keep it from falling out. I'd had a bacon sandwich, but he'd taken bacon, eggs, sausages, beans and toast, and lots of it.

I had to ask Bee to repeat everything.

'Team Tribe are in the lead. There's an award ceremony at the end of the week.' (I didn't realise the whole week was a competition.) 'But there are points for other things, not just the challenges, like helping, and using common sense.' She took a mouthful of beans on a square of bread, and carried on. 'Today is a day of two halves. Four groups are starting the day doing raft building, then they swap with the other four groups and do wood collecting and campfire building.'

I was a bit surprised by how much I was looking forward to it all. Why had I thought camp would be awful? I wasn't missing home one bit.

'What are *we* doing?'

'Tribe are raft building first. And so are the Missiles, worst luck. So, we have to clear away, bathroom stop, then meet back at the mess tent in wellies.'

We left Copper Pie troughing and got ready.

Land
Ahoy

Max and Mr Morris seemed to be our raft building instructors, although it didn't look like Mr Morris was going to be much help in his jacket and tie. Max took us up river, where it was much wider, and gave each team an area to work in – he called it a station. (But no trains in sight.) Each team had four blue plastic barrels, loads of rope and a pile of wooden planks, all different sizes. Callum's 'station' was next to ours.

'OK, teams. It's a race. Who's going to build a raft that floats well enough to carry your whole team across the river? No rules, except no fighting, no cheating, no stealing, and no feet on the riverbed. Off you go!'

Awesome. I couldn't wait to get started. I had the most fantastic idea, right away.

'This is easy, we need to make the barrels the four corners and then use the wood to . . .'

No one was listening. They were all messing about. I tried again. 'Listen, if we have a barrel at each corner —'

'No, let's see if we can make a snake-shape raft,' said Bee.

'Or a star,' said Lily.

'Let's not bother with the barrels and make a totally wooden raft, you know, all strapped together with rope, like we've been stranded on a desert island and have to escape before we starve.' Fifty's contribution – a bit dramatic as usual.

'We'll all end up in the water anyway,' said Copper Pie. 'Let's not bother.'

At least Jonno was taking it seriously. 'Go on with your idea, Keener.'

I waited until all five of them were looking *and* listening and then I went through my idea. It was obvious really. The raft needed to float, but also it needed to be balanced, symmetrical. I'm not sure why, I just knew that was best. I mapped it out on the grass using bits of wood. Jonno suggested we have diagonals to help the structure. We added some in. It looked good. *All we needed to do was tie a few good knots*, I thought.

'Shall we get on with it then?' said Bee, nodding at the plan.

'Hey! Quit spying, Callum.' Fifty jumped up and tried

128

to stand in the way of our blueprint for the raft. Pity he wasn't taller.

'Go away, Hog,' said Copper Pie. He gave our number one enemy a shove to make sure the message was clear.

Callum tried to look as though he didn't care and strolled back to the Missiles.

That was all that Team Tribe needed to get us going – the thought that Callum's team might beat us with our own design. Even Copper Pie, who thought we were going to sink whatever, was sorting through the woodpile to find the right length planks. Jonno and I were the knotters, and raft management. Fifty and Copper Pie were choosers, fetchers and carriers. Bee and Lily were rope substitutes (they held things in place until they got secured) . . . no, they were scaffolding – sounds better. What a team! It took longer than I thought, and the knots were difficult because plastic barrels are slippy, but we were still the first to tell Max we were ready to launch.

He came over for a quick inspection, and suggested we add a couple more strips of wood at right angles to the main planks to make the structure more solid. We did it in a hurry, desperate to get on the river.

'All ready, Mr Max,' said Lily. She saluted – girls can be a bit odd.

Max shouted, making us all jump. 'Mr Morris, over here. We have our first contender for the river crossing.' And then, 'Can all the teams stop for a second and come and watch Tribe's first attempt.' I was glad he'd dropped the '+ Lily' bit of our name.

The other kids came over. I had a look around to see how they'd got on. Two of the teams had tried to put the four barrels in the middle – bit random. Team GB didn't seem to have done anything at all. I looked back at ours. I had confidence running through my veins like blood (I got that from a song my sister listens to, except the word's 'lightning', not 'confidence').

The sun was making the water glitter. It wasn't very far across to the other side. We were bound to make it if we pushed off hard enough.

'Come on then,' said Max. 'We're all waiting.'

As we carried our raft to the edge, I realised we didn't have a plan for how to get on board. I whispered to Jonno.

'Two at a time,' he said. 'And we have to keep low, maybe crawl on.'

I deliberately didn't look at Callum. If I was going to have to crawl I didn't want his face smirking at me, hoping I'd fail.

Jonno turned to the others. 'Keener and I are going on first. Do the same as us, stay low, OK?'

I was starting to feel a little bit nervous, but there wasn't time to think about it. We pushed the raft on to the water. Fifty and Copper Pie stayed on the bank and held it steady while Jonno and I crawled on. It wobbled madly, I heard some gasps from the audience, but we both instinctively went flat on our bellies, which worked. The raft calmed down. I tried to think of it as a surfboard.

'There's no room for us,' said Fifty. (Of the six of us, he was the one who didn't want to fall in.) So we wriggled, still on our bellies, to the outside edges so that Fifty and Copper Pie could slide on in the middle. So far so good. C.P. came my side and Fifty went Jonno's side, to balance the weight. Two to go, and no room . . .

'What shall we do?' said Bee.

No answer.

'Coming on board,' said Lily. I turned my head to see Lily grab Bee's hand and clamber on to the raft. I felt her knee crash into me, forcing a gap between me and Copper Pie. The raft lurched, my arms went up to my elbows in water, but amazingly someone must have counterbalanced it. Bee, I supposed. It took a few seconds to settle down, and you couldn't exactly say we were floating, but we weren't sinking . . . yet.

I think people were laughing, some might have even been yelling instructions, but it was all a jumble.

'Do little paddles,' said Jonno.

I moved my arms backwards and forwards. The raft moved too, in every direction except forwards.

'Lily and Bee, can you paddle?' Jonno asked.

They both leaned over, which was nearly the end of us. Fifty squealed.

'No way. We can't reach the water,' said Bee.

'But you could kick, Copper Pie,' said Lily.

'But I've got shoes on,' he said.

'What does that matter? And anyway they're wellies,' said Bee.

A few dangerous wobbles later, I'd moved forwards and was gripping the front of the raft with my head sticking way out over the water, same as Jonno, to help balance Fifty and Copper Pie who had wriggled backwards so that their heads and bodies were on the raft, but their legs were dangling in the river. Bee and Lily were kneeling, desperately trying to keep the balance every time one of us moved. If it hadn't been so tense, it would have been funny. I can't imagine what we looked like, although there were plenty of photos being taken by Mr Morris, so I guessed I was going to find out.

It was slow, and our path wasn't exactly straight, but with Copper Pie and Fifty kicking with their feet, and me and Jonno paddling with our hands, we made our way across. Jonno and I even managed to get off the raft the other side without the water going over our wellies. Unfortunately that meant the raft tipped. Bee and Lily managed to scramble off but Fifty and Copper Pie got soaked. They didn't care (I don't think). We were too busy celebrating. *Team Tribe was without doubt the most superb team ever to build a raft,* I thought.

And that's exactly what Max said. He said in all the years he'd worked at Highwoods never before had a team got across on their first try. Wow! Double wow, in fact.

We watched the other teams try and try again with their useless rafts. Callum had given up. His lot had a go at copying our design but it still didn't work. They didn't even manage to get on it, let alone float. I think his team had a row after that. Jonno said we should offer to help but we all sat on him, so that was the end of that idea.

Eventually, the We Hate Spiders team actually got all six of them on the water, attached to the raft. Four of them were lying on the barrels with their legs dangling in the water (it was the only way they could stay stable), but Max decided that as long as their feet didn't touch the bottom it was allowed. They basically swam across, but they got a massive clap anyway.

In the time left before lunch we messed about on two-man kayaks. It was an all-round top morning.

'Does anyone want to help build the bonfire this afternoon?' asked Max.

'Yes. Absolutely. Me.' Fifty wanted to make sure he got on fire-making duty.

'Yes, please,' said Jonno.

'All right,' said Copper Pie.

I think Team Tribe must have been the only team that heard as no one else volunteered. All four teams were walking back to the field, having dismantled our rafts so that the afternoon lot could have a go, but we were at the front. (Obeying Camp Rule No. 5 – to be the advance party.)

'I thought we were all collecting wood for the bonfire?' said Bee.

'That's right,' said Max, 'but I'll need some of you to help me get the structure right. You can't just bung a pile of wood into a heap. There's an art to a decent bonfire.'

'Is the wood coming from over there?' asked Lily. She pointed at the dark forest behind us.

'It is. So it won't just be a case of collecting it. Transporting it will be a challenge in itself.'

Jonno looked over at the wood. 'Actually, I'd like to go to the woods . . . if that's OK?'

'I'll be a campfire builder,' said Bee.

'Same,' said Fifty. 'I'm good at fires.' He reached into his pocket and pulled out his firesteel and made a couple of sparks.

'We can use that to start the fire if you like, Fifty,' said Max.

Fifty was in heaven. Fires. He loves fires (and Probably Rose and sugar).

'What about you, Keener?' Max asked me. He was good at names. He knew all of us already.

'I'm for the woods,' I said.

'And you, Lily?'

'Woods too,' she said.

'So Bee, Copper Pie and Fifty, are you my helpers?'

'We are,' said Fifty, with a massive smile on his face.

'Good.'

We went off for lunch. I was hungry as a hippo, to quote my dad. As I ate my ham roll I realised I hadn't told the others about the Tribers' Camp Rules, so they didn't know we were about to break one. The one that said we should 'stick together'.

The
Woods

Fifty didn't need a lesson in how to build a fire. He gave Max a lesson. On my first trip back from the woods, dragging a heap of wood tied in a bundle behind me, the fire team were all sitting cross-legged listening to Fifty's lecture.

FIFTY'S CAMPFIRE
IN 10 EASY STEPS

1. You need a spark to start the fire, from matches or a firesteel.
2. Collect small dry sticks, bits of bark, and dry leaves (called tinder).
3. Collect kindling – slightly bigger sticks and twigs.

---

4. Collect fuel – that means big bits of wood that will make the fire last longer because they take ages to burn. It has to be dead wood from the ground. Live stuff still attached to the tree is too wet.

5. Use rocks to make a ring to keep the fire from spreading.

6. Make a pile of the tinder.

7. Make a teepee around the pile using the kindling.

8. Build four square walls around the teepee using longer pieces with gaps between them. This makes a chimney.

9. Carry on adding wood in a teepee shape, but leave a way in so you can still reach the tinder to light the fire.

10. Light it!

'You forgot something, Fifty,' said Max. Fifty looked a bit puzzled. 'Putting out a fire. Making the area safe so no one gets burnt and it doesn't relight.'

Copper Pie, Lily, Bee and me all laughed – Fifty isn't interested in putting them out. The laughing stopped pretty quickly though as Max had something else to say in a deadly serious voice. 'Never start a fire without an adult present. Never think of fire as a toy.' He wasn't just staring at Fifty, he was drilling a direct channel into the centre of Fifty's brain.

Fifty nodded.

Max sent me off to find tinder. Jonno was put in charge of kindling. The other two teams (Missiles and We Hate Spiders) were on fuel – we needed lots of fuel. The other lucky team (Team GB) got to go down on the beach and collect driftwood.

The nurse who wasn't a nurse stayed up in the woods. She was 'supervising' us to make sure there was no tree climbing, no wandering away from the group, no lots-of-other-stuff-I-didn't-listen-to. I was more interested in the problem of transportation. I needed a bucket to collect the tinder. It was too small to hold. And there was a limit to how much I could get in my pockets.

'Jonno, what can I use to collect the small stuff for the fire?'

He looked around. Was he expecting to see a basket, or a great big plastic bag hanging from a tree?

'How about a huge piece of bark?' he said.

Good idea, I thought. He helped me peel off a long curved bit, like a piece of guttering. I filled it with dry leaves, twigs and more bark and held it with one end against my tummy and the other end in the air, so none of it fell out. We had to tell the nurse person every time we went back down to camp, so that's what I did.

Jonno came down a few minutes later. He'd used the

same idea to carry the kindling.

'Good lads,' said Max. There was quite a pile of wood that the others had collected, neatly stacked in size order. Lily and Bee seemed to be in charge of that. A few of the kids were having a rest – they'd obviously lugged too much heavy wood. Fifty was busy with Max, chatting, and Copper Pie was laying a stone circle. Made me feel a bit spooked, as though evil sprits might dance in it while we were asleep. I left them to it and went back up to the wood.

Get Me Out of the Woods

'Hi, Keener.' It was the friendly girl from the bus. She was looking straight at me so I had to say something back.

'Hi.'

'It's nice here, isn't it?' she said.

'Yeah.'

I tried to walk off, but she came with me. I could see the other We-Hate-Spiders girls were with the nurse person a bit further into the wood. The Missiles were nowhere to be seen. That meant we were alone, me and her. *Yelp!* I bent down to gather up some more leaves for the tinder. *One more bark full would be enough*, I thought. *Then I could escape.*

'I could help you, if you like.'

'I'm fine, thanks.' I scooped up some general leaf and stick mess. I had a horrible idea that wouldn't go away. I thought maybe she *liked* me, if you know what I mean.

I picked up my bit of gutter, in a hurry to get away, and a load of the tinder slid towards the other end. She grabbed it, and stopped the whole lot from ending up back on the ground where it started.

'It'll be easier if we carry an end each,' she said. She was right, but that didn't mean I wanted to go along with it. I wanted her to leave me alone. I wanted to run back down the hill and find a Triber. I wanted Jonno to come back up to get more kindling and frighten her off.

But I said, 'OK.'

Possibly the worst five minutes of my life began. Me and no-name friendly girl carried the bark between us, adding more stuff until it was full. She kept trying to talk to me, and I kept trying not to answer so she'd go away. My face was the raspberry pink that it goes in times of dire embarrassment. I was sweating, on the inside and outside, if that's possible. I knew that any second I was going to be spotted, with a girl (Bee and Lily don't count), and there would be teasing . . . for ever. I had to get away.

'Thanks for helping. I'll take it down,' I said. I tried to yank it out of her hands as I said it, but she held on.

'I'll come too,' she said.

NO! NO! NO!

An idea catapulted through the state of emergency in my brain.

'You can't leave your team,' I said. I gave the gutter-shaped bark a really determined yank. She stumbled a bit, but still didn't let it go. What she did was a whole lot worse. She shouted, loudly, over towards the rest of her group and the nurse lady.

'Can I help Keener take the tinder down to the campfire?'

The nurse looked over at us. 'Yes, Zoe, go ahead.'

Oh dear! An even worse five minutes of my life seemed unavoidable.

Zoe started walking, still chatting to me. I was dragged along behind her, holding on to the end of the gutter like a puppy on a lead. I watched her biscuit-coloured ponytail swing from side to side. *Come on brain!* I couldn't arrive at the camp with *Zoe* in full view of everyone.

We came out into the bright sunshine. I had about four minutes until my life changed. Four minutes until the whole of the fire team, and all the kids lying about down by the mess tent, saw me and Zoe TOGETHER. In my head I could already hear them singing that rubbish rhyme:

Zoe and Keener sitting in the tree
K-I-S-S-I-N-G
First comes love
Then comes marriage
Then comes Zoe with a baby carriage.

I trudged behind her wondering why she'd picked me, and wishing she hadn't.

'Hey, Keener,' said Jonno. He was coming up the hill, his

emptied-out bark slung over his shoulder.

'Jonno!' I said, really pleased to see him. I stared over the top of his glasses into his eyes, trying to send a message: *Save me, save me.*

'Hi,' said Zoe.

I knew what you were meant to do. Mum says you must always introduce people if you know them both but they don't know each other. *No way was I doing that.*

'Hi, Zoe,' said Jonno. *No need anyway.*

Jonno looked as though he was going to carry on walking. *Didn't he realise I needed saving?*

'Why don't you come down with me, Jonno?' I said. 'I was going to ask if we're allowed to go and get some wood from the beach.'

'OK,' he said. Excellent! *Surely that would get rid of Zoe.*

I turned to face her. 'Jonno can help me now.'

She smiled again. 'But I want to come to the beach with you.'

I'm not proud of what I did next. But you have to understand, I couldn't spend the rest of my time at camp with everyone giggling about me, and trying to get me and Zoe to sit together and all the other rubbish that goes on when there's a boy-girl thing.

'Grab this.' I thrust my end of the bark at Jonno. 'I forgot something. You go down, I'll catch you up,' and disappeared back into the wood. Fast. I didn't look behind me. I went back to the clearing where I'd collected the tinder, saw the other We Hate Spiders coming towards me dragging bundled fuel and decided I needed some time out. I saw a climbable-looking tree and in a second, I was up it.

Tent
Talk

I stayed in the tree until there was no one left in the wood, which was quite a long time. The Spider group went away but Jonno and Zoe came back up – I guess they weren't allowed to join the beach crew – and got some big wood. Then Callum's group came up too. I stayed where I was, perched like a bird, but not chirping. I wondered whether Jonno was going to be cross. Probably not, I decided, because he and Zoe were chatting away. Maybe he *liked* her, if you get me.

When the last wood-collectors had left and no one else seemed to be coming I got down, grabbed an armful of twigs, more kindling than tinder, and strolled down to the campfire.

It looked great, all ready for tomorrow night. A giant teepee shape, with what looked like a doorway on one side to get in. I knew what that was – a tunnel to reach the middle and light the tinder.

I joined the other Tribers (and Lily). Zoe had gone off to her team. *Phew!* We chatted, and amazingly no one asked me where I'd been so that was cool . . . until tucked-up-in-tent time, when Jonno spilled the beans.

'I saw you in the tree, Keener.'

The raspberry pink came again but it was dark so it didn't matter.

'Sorry,' I said. 'But I had a shadow.'

'And you gave her to me,' said Jonno. 'Thanks!'

'*Keen-er's got a girl-friend*,' sang Fifty.

I kicked him, with my sleeping-bag legs. 'That's exactly why I offloaded her on Jonno,' I said.

'Bit lame,' said Fifty. 'Dumping on a mate.'

There was no answer to that. Except . . . You're right, I'm lame.

'Shut up about girls,' said Copper Pie. 'Let's work out how to *win*.'

'How to win what?' I said, glad to change the subject.

'Everything,' said Copper Pie.

'He means the best team at camp. We're in the lead with two days to go, shouldn't be too hard,' said Fifty.

'What's left to do?' I said.

'The campfire,' said Fifty.

'That's tomorrow night,' I said. 'And you can't *win* the campfire.'

'There's the assault course,' said Jonno.

'No worries,' said Copper Pie.

There was a silence. I don't know what the others were thinking but I know what I was – Fifty was never going to get over the wall, and even if he did, he wasn't going to do the monkey bars over the river crossing.

'We'll help you, Fifty,' said Jonno. 'That's the whole point of being a team.'

'Thanks,' said Fifty.

'I could kick you over the wall,' said our redheaded football fiend.

'That's sorted then,' said Jonno. We all laughed. But we weren't laughing the next day.

A Great Way to Start the Day

Breakfast was delicious. A bacon sandwich sitting outside with your mates is the best. And as a treat there was a huge urn full of hot chocolate. Even Copper Pie's suction method of food consumption didn't ruin it.

Max gave us a rundown of the day, as usual. We were bodyboarding in the morning – yes, yes, yes! And it was the assault course in the afternoon. We were in two halves again: us, the Spiders, Callum's lot and Team GB. *Bring it on!*

The water was heaven. I'd already caught three waves before anyone else was up to their knees. It helped that I'd brought my own wetsuit – there were a lot of kids fiddling with zips and moaning that the suits were too tight around the neck. The waves weren't cooking (like the day Dad took all the

Tribers to Woolacombe) but they were plenty big enough to take you on a ride all the way to the shore. Bee and Jonno came out to join me. And so did Max, the instructor.

'Keener, I hear you're a wicked longboarder – well, I'm afraid you have to stay in your depth while you're here with me.'

'You'll have to tell Marco the same thing,' I said, paddling back to where I could just about stand. 'He's Off the Richter.' (It means awesome.)

Even though Copper Pie and Fifty didn't go out that far, Tribe was way better than everyone else. In fact we took pity on the Spiders (well, Jonno did and I was standing next to him) and gave them some coaching. I didn't mind. It's easy to teach someone how to catch a wave. They all had their weight too far back on the board. The tip needs to be down, whether it's a surfboard or a bodyboard. I did all the demonstrating and Jonno did the talking. Suited me.

The friendly girl, Zoe, stood next to Jonno while he explained all the stuff he'd learnt when we went together. Me and Fifty winked at each other. Copper Pie saw too, and next thing he'd mown into them on his board. (It didn't hurt, they're soft boards.) I think he was rescuing Jonno. Whether Jonno wanted rescuing – who knows?

The morning went too quickly. The sea was warm (for England) and the sun was hot and I loved catching the waves with the others. We came in all in a row a few times – a wall of Tribers landing on the beach together.

'You've all done this before,' said Max.

We nodded.

'The Spiders are getting the hang of it too,' said Jonno.

'Yes,' said Max. 'I saw you helping them.'

We were so going to win. Best at bodyboarding. Best at helping. *Go Tribe!*

Lunch was hot dogs. I ate and ate and ate. I didn't eat as much as Copper Pie, but that would have put me at the Guinness Book of Records level. Afterwards, Max said it was free time until two o'clock. I wanted to go back down to the beach but Max reckoned otherwise.

'Have a rest. Play cards or something.'

We're not playing-cards people – we dragged our sleeping bags out on to the grass and laid in the sun, telling ghost stories to try and scare each other.

THE HAUNTED POCKET
BY FIFTY

The boy sat down on the swing. The park was empty. No one came there in the evenings. He put his head in his hands. The swing gave a little squeak and he jumped. 'Leave me alone,' he said out loud.

'Nooooo,' said the voice. The boy jumped again. He would never escape. He knew that. He was being haunted, and he hated it, and he was scared of it, and no one believed him.

It was chilly, as the sun had gone down. The boy blew on his hands and then put his left hand in his pocket. ' Weeeeee,' shouted the ghost. He pulled his hand out as fast as he could. There was a burn mark on his palm.

'Leave me alone,' said the boy again.

'Neeeveeer,' said the voice. The boy was fed up. Fed up with battling his pocket ghost.

'What do you want from me?' said the boy, desperately.

'Sugar,' was the answer. 'Glorious sugar.'

The boy reached into his rucksack and pulled out a pack of three bourbon biscuits. He fed them to his pocket. The pocket was quiet for a while. The boy left the park and wandered home. He'd tried changing jackets, wearing clothes with no pockets, but it was always there, stealing his sweets. He was doomed.

It didn't work, because the stories were rubbish and the sun was too bright.

'Hey Bee,' said Jonno. He was lying on his back with his eyes shut. 'Haven't noticed you sleepwalking this week. Thought it was your speciality.'

Bee propped herself up on one elbow. She had a smug look on her face. 'I'm cured,' she said. She reached into her pocket and pulled out Fifty's flower remedy. It was obviously good stuff. I thought I'd get him to give me some. *Who knows what it could cure?*

The camp horn sounded which meant it was time for the afternoon activity. We followed Max and Mr Morris (who was wearing red trousers and a short-sleeved khaki shirt, which was at least better than a jacket and tie).

'We're going to walk the course first. I'll point out the possible pitfalls. Then it's a relay, in pairs. The first pair goes off on the sound of my gun.' He shot it and we all jumped. 'The second pair go off when they hear the gun again, which will mean one pair has reached the other end. The third pair wait for the third shot.'

'That's not fair,' said Bee. 'Why should all the second pairs go off at the same time? Why can't —'

'I didn't say it was fair. I said that's what we're doing,' said Max. That shut her up.

I was next to Fifty, who was concentrating really hard on everything Max said. I could tell he was worried he wasn't going to make it over all the obstacles. I'll describe the course: a high wall with a drop the other side, a rope bridge, a pole to climb followed by a zip wire over the river, scramble nets to crawl under, a slippery slope to get up, ropes to swing on, a balance beam, then a ladder leading up to monkey bars back over the river, and then a jump on to the bank – or a drop into the river!

'You'll be fine,' I said.

Fifty stared back at me. His face was as white as chalk and his black curly hair looked even blacker, like he'd been monochromed.

'Course I will,' he said, '. . . and there goes a flying pig.'

The Race
Is On

'OK,' said Max. 'So, divide your team into pairs, number them one, two, three and send your first pair to the start line. Double quick.'

We all looked at each other.

'I'll go with Lily,' said Bee.

'Not a great idea,' said Copper Pie. 'Two girls together . . .'

'Says who?' said Bee.

There was a delay, while Copper Pie worked out the right answer. 'No one,' he said.

'And why don't you go with Fifty, Copper Pie?' said Bee.

'OK,' he said. I thought I should go with Fifty but Jonno said, 'So it's me and Keener,' and that was that.

'We'll be pair one,' said Bee. 'OK, Lily?'

'Sure.'

They lined up next to Callum and Jamie, Zoe and her partner, and two boys from Team GB.

'Go Tribe!' shouted Copper Pie.

Callum turned and sneered. 'No chance,' he said.

'We'll see,' said Copper Pie back to him.

'In your dreams, Ginge.'

Callum was pushing his luck. If Max hadn't sounded his gun we might have had a *situation*.

Bee and Lily shot over the wall in the lead. Bee gave Lily a leg up and then Lily leant down and grabbed Bee's arm and she scampered up the wall like a lizard. They disappeared after that, and we had to wait until they got to the pole to spot them again. At the top of the pole was a platform to catch the zip over to the other side of the river. Callum and Jamie were there first so Bee and Lily had to wait. Really annoying. But Bee and Lily managed to get ahead under the scramble nets. They were like snakes, gliding below the mesh without getting caught on anything. We all clapped and shouted when they emerged at the other end and started to make their way up the slippery slope. It was greasy, like it had washing-up liquid on it. Bee nearly got to the top by crawling on all fours but then she stood up and slid all the way back down. Lily learnt from that and stayed crouched until the top. Oh no, everyone was catching up! All eight of them were on the slope.

Bee and Lily made it to the top and grabbed a rope just before one of the Spiders.

'Whee!' shouted Bee.

'We're coming in first,' said Copper Pie. 'Get ready for the gun, Keener, and you, Jonno.'

Jonno did a thumbs up. I could feel my pulse getting quicker. I didn't want to let the side down – if the girls could do it, so could I.

The balancing beam looked easy, but the monkey bars looked really difficult. Bee didn't bother with the first few, she just reached out and grabbed the third or maybe fourth rung (they were actually ladders laid horizontally – four in a row). Lily was on the one next to Bee, and then there was Callum, and two seconds later, Jamie.

'Go, Bee! Go, Lily!' I shouted my head off.

Bee finished with the most amazing jump, by swinging her legs back and then throwing her legs up and forward like a gymnast on those parallel bar things. The rest of her body followed and she was first, two feet slammed down on to the bank. Callum landed next. I was half watching them arrive back on our side of the river and half waiting for the shot. It didn't come, because a complete pair had to land before the next ones could go.

Lily was dangling halfway across the river. Bee yelled, 'Come on, Lily. Move your arm.' Lily whimpered, and dropped into the water. It wasn't far, but it was wet. She waded across, up to her waist. Jamie was struggling too but Callum's shouting made him do it. They both touched the grassy edge at the same time. Equal first.

BANG!

We were off.

Doing it was completely different to watching other people do it. It was all so fast. I was scrambling up, then down, then across, then on my belly, then at an angle, then balancing and then we were at the monkey bars. It was neck and neck all the way – I could hear loud panting but I didn't know if it was me or someone else, we were all so close together. We all ended up at the ladders within nanoseconds of each other, so each pair bagsied a ladder. Jonno went in front of me. He's not that sporty but he had no problem swinging like an orangutan across the water. I was right behind. My armpit skin was stretched so far I reckoned I'd have to fold it under my arm at the end, but I'd decided before I even started that I was definitely making it to the other side, so I did. The shot for the last pair to get going rang out the minute I landed, sweating, panting and doubled-over with stitch. Jonno elbowed me – I think it meant 'well done'. Neither of us could actually speak.

I straightened up as soon as I could to see how Fifty and Copper Pie were getting on. They'd got past the wall, which was good – Copper Pie obviously hadn't had to kick Fifty over. I waited for them to appear by the pole, ready to zip over the river. The Spiders got there first, then the pair from the Missiles. *Where were the Tribers?* I was pretty sure Copper Pie would make sure Fifty got through, but it didn't stop me worrying. Team GB started climbing up the pole.

We were last, wherever we were. I wondered how Max was going to judge it. Bee and Lily were equal first out of their race. Me and Jonno were first. If Copper Pie and Fifty were last, what would the overall position be?

By the time Fifty (all red-faced and sweaty, and still small of course) had reached the scramble nets there was no hope. They were too far behind. Although Copper Pie didn't seem to know that – he was still doing his best to catch up. He lifted the netting by arching his back to let Fifty scuttle through in super-quick time. Then he sprinted towards the slope and his speed seemed to counteract the slipperiness, and somehow Fifty kept up with him, stride for stride, like a mini-shadow. They swung on the ropes and galloped across the beam. Only the monkey bars left. Team GB was already home but the Spiders and Missiles were only just starting the ladders. *Come on, Tribe!*

An Assault on Tribe

I don't want to think about what happened next. It was too awful.

Copper Pie threw himself at the ladders, grabbed a rung with one hand, then the next and the next and then he was on the bank with us. He'd overtaken the two other pairs . . . but Fifty was left behind on the other side. He hadn't even tried to climb the ladder and get on to the bars.

'Come on, Fifty!' shouted Bee, but he just stood there, looking down at the water. I knew he wasn't going to do it. He didn't want to fall in, and he didn't want to wade because the water had been waist-high on Lily, so it would be armpit-high on Fifty. I wished Copper Pie had waited for him. I wished I'd been Fifty's partner. I wouldn't have gone off, I'd have helped him over . . . somehow.

Fifty looked across at us. I tried to make an encouraging face, but he shook his head.

'Loser!' shouted Callum.

'None of that,' said Max, in a voice that really meant it. Callum shut up.

'Forget the monkey bars, go through the water,' yelled Lily. She didn't get how much he hates the thought of being out of his depth. When we went surfing he didn't go in past his knees.

Max didn't get it either. 'Fifty. If you don't want to do the monkey bars, just wade across. It's fine. But a bit wet . . .' He laughed, as though getting wet was no big deal. Somehow that made it worse.

Fifty didn't answer. He just stood there. I felt really uncomfortable, like maybe we should go and get him. That would be better than doing nothing. I was going to suggest it but . . .

Lily was getting impatient. 'Fifty! Stop mucking about and get over here.' She grinned at the rest of us, like we were lollipop ladies stopping the traffic and she was a mum waiting for a naughty toddler who wouldn't come. You can tell she's not a Triber, not one of us. We all knew he couldn't do it. We all knew it was a crisis. What we didn't know was how it was all going to end.

Jonno walked over to Max and said quietly, 'I'm going to go and help him. He doesn't really like the water.'

Max made a face – maybe he'd never heard of someone

not liking water, or maybe he couldn't work out how Fifty could do the raft challenge on the water but not this one.

'Oh, OK. I'll sort him out.'

Deadly embarrassing. In front of our half of the camp: Missiles, Team GB, Spiders and us, Max went to get Fifty, striding straight through the water as though it was a puddle. The minute Max was out of hearing Callum started up again.

'Pride, I mean Tribe, comes before a fall.' He looked around, enjoying being mean. 'Not exactly a water baby, is he? Just a regular baby. D'you call him the Tribe weed? Little wee-eed.'

'Say anything else and you're in the water, Hog,' said Copper Pie.

Callum stared straight back at him. 'Weeee-eeed!' he said.

Oh no! Here we go! Copper Pie took two paces forward and shoved Callum really hard in the chest. There were a few seconds of cartoon-like wobbling while Callum tried to stop himself falling backwards and then a splash.

I checked to see what Max was about to do, but he'd disappeared, as had Fifty. At least that bought us some time. Jonno must have been thinking the same thing – he was already by the river stretching out an arm to try and help Callum up the bank. Callum didn't take it though. He clambered up on his own, dripping.

'You'll be sent home,' said Callum, staring at Copper Pie.

'Yeah,' said Jamie.

'For pushing another kid into the river.'

'Yeah,' said Jamie.

'And we've got . . .' Callum looked around. 'Twenty witnesses.'

'Twenty witnesses who would be more than happy to repeat all the things you said about Fifty,' said Jonno. 'I mean, I'm sure you were only joking, but it sounded a whole lot like bullying to me.'

Jonno does it again, I thought. He should work for the United Nations, stopping wars before they happen.

Callum kind of snarled. But when Max whizzed back over the river on the zip, came up to us and said, 'Looking a bit wet, there, Callum,' Callum didn't say a word. Max raised his eyebrows – I think he probably guessed there'd been a *situation*. I think he probably didn't want to know anything about it though. Suited us.

'Keener and Jonno, can you walk back down to the mess tent? We'll follow in a bit.'

Everyone knew that must mean Fifty had gone back to base. Everyone knew Tribe'd failed to complete the assault course, and Fifty was chicken. It was not Tribe's greatest moment. And it wasn't Fifty's. I couldn't wait to see him – to tell him it was OK. There was more to being brave than crossing a bit of water. Fifty had spent every year since Reception being big even though he was the littlest. He'd never once given in, even though sometimes it was harder for him. I mean, half the time he couldn't even see the film in the cinema without sitting on the arm. I wanted to see him. Being a Triber, or being a friend, isn't about being a certain size or getting across a river or up a tree or catching a wave. It's nothing to do with what you can do, it's about who you are.

Matters

Jonno was better at it than me, even though I've been friends with Fifty for longer (for ever in fact). Jonno said it didn't matter that we didn't win, and it didn't matter that Fifty didn't do the monkey bars and it didn't matter that Callum and Jamie would never let Tribe forget its complete and utter failure at the assault course. (He didn't use those exact words.) 'Nothing matters,' Jonno said, 'except that we're Tribe, and Callum's not.'

What Fifty said was, 'It matters to me.'

I said nothing.

Eventually, all the other kids from the assault course came back. Bee and Copper Pie headed straight for us.

'It doesn't matter,' said Bee. 'Everyone's frightened of something. And with me it's birds. That's more stupid

164

than being afraid of monkey bars.'

'It wasn't the monkey bars,' I said. 'It was the water underneath he didn't like.'

'Whatever,' said Bee. 'It's still better than being frightened of flapping wings.' She shuddered. Copper Pie started flapping. She ran in circles and he flapped after her. It was lunatic but it did the trick. Jonno flapped and squawked too, so I joined in. It was better than staring at Fifty. When the chicken dance was over, the subject was over too. We talked about the campfire, and what we might be doing on our last day. I couldn't believe we were already near the end. It had gone in a flash. Fifty was quiet. We all noticed, but didn't know how to turn up his volume. Maybe it would turn itself up when he stopped going over and over that awful moment on the bank.

Campfire's Burning

Fifty didn't want to light the fire. Unheard of. He lent Max his firesteel and Max picked Zoe to light it. She had to crawl into the tunnel to reach the tinder and kindling in the centre. It was a good design. She had a few tries before she could get the spark, but once she'd worked it out the flames caught right away and in no time it was burning well. We'd had tea and were all ready with our marshmallows on sticks for pudding. The Tribers sat in a line with Fifty in the middle, like we were trying to protect him. Callum kept glancing over our way and smiling a sickly smile. He loved the fact that Fifty had failed.

We sang songs while we ate the sticky (and bit burnt) marshmallows. I'm not much of a singer but I joined in – it was hard not to. Max changed lots of the words so we had lines like:

They scraped Ed off the tarmac like a lump of strawberry jam

Then rolled him up in Bee's kitbag and sent him home to mum

and

Oh you'll never get to heaven, in a Missiles' boat
Cos the gosh darn thing, won't even float

And

Oh you'll never get to heaven, on a Spiders' bike
Cos you'll get halfway, then you'll have to hike.

We finished off with hot chocolate and camp cake, made by Flower Power (looked terrible, tasted delicious). I tried to get Fifty talking but he wasn't interested. I knew what he was doing, because it was what I'd have done. He was going through it all in his mind again and again, wishing he'd had a go. Wishing he wasn't the only kid that didn't even try to cross the river. A few girls fell in, but at least they tried.

By the time we put out the fire (and made sure there was no possibility of loose sparks by dousing it with river water) we were all desperate to get in our sleeping bags.

There was no chatting in the tent. I don't know why the others were quiet but I know why I was. I was worried that if we started talking we'd end up discussing the failed river crossing, and as we'd already tried to convince Fifty that it didn't matter, and hadn't succeeded, I didn't relish the idea of having another go. I mean, as soon as we got back home it would be forgotten by everyone (*except* Callum – but Tribe'd find a way to silence him).

I don't remember thinking anything else. I didn't dream. I didn't hear anyone snore or feel anyone's knee or elbow as they wriggled in their cocoons. I slept like I was dead. And woke up suddenly when I heard Jonno's voice.

'Where's Fifty? Where's Fifty?'

There's
Fifty

The camp horn sounded before I had a chance to find out what was going on. It gave three eardrum-shattering blasts, two more than normal.

'What's going on?' I said, eyes open but not working. I sat up, pulled down my 'jama top which was wedged under my armpits and focussed on Jonno, who was looking in Fifty's sleeping bag.

'Fifty's missing,' he said.

'Let me see,' said Copper Pie. He didn't seem to think Jonno had looked properly. Fifty might be small but he's not so small you wouldn't spot him in the bottom of a sleeping bag. Copper Pie shook his head. I could hear other kids moving about and talking outside. The camp horn wasn't the sort of thing you could sleep through.

'Better get dressed,' I said. Jonno was ahead of me. Joggers on, hoodie pulled over his T-shirt. No shoes.

'I'm going to see what's happening.'

I rushed to catch up. I wasn't sure whether I was meant to be worried about Fifty or assume he'd gone to the washrooms, worried about why the camp horn had gone so early or excited . . . *it might mean early morning bodyboarding!* Copper Pie and I stuck our heads out of the flap at the same time, and a nanosecond later there was Bee's. She said Lily was still asleep – amazing.

'What's going on?' said Bee.

'No idea,' I said.

'Fifty's missing,' said Copper Pie.

'Is that why the horn sounded?' she said.

'No. No one knows yet,' I said.

'Do you think he ran away?' said Bee.

I hadn't thought of that. Maybe he disappeared in the night and tried to hitch home and got mown down by an articulated lorry.

'No way,' said Copper Pie. 'Too chicken.'

'Who are you calling chicken?' said Jonno, running towards us. 'Come and see.' He about-turned as soon as he had our attention, and ran back where he'd come from. We followed. And the rest of camp wasn't far behind us. It was like we were rats and Jonno was the Pied Piper, but without the music.

We chased after him to the bank of the river and then he

THE PIED PIPER,
AND WHY IT'S STUPID

The town was full of rats. The townspeople wanted to get rid of them. They tried cats and poison, but neither worked. They didn't try bombs, sleeping gas, foxes, a steamroller or the giant pitcher plant. The giant pitcher plant has sweet, tasty nectar that attracts animals and if they're small enough, like rats or shrews, they fall in and are trapped. The acid inside dissolves the rats. Job done.

Anyway, the Pied Piper played a tune that made the rats follow him into the river and they all drowned. But, the townspeople refused to pay the Piper the money they'd agreed. So the Piper piped a tune that kiddies liked and they all followed him and they died too. But, why didn't the townies take the pipe off the Piper? Or give all the children earplugs? Or put an enormous ice-cream van in the town and make it all free? Surely most kids would choose ice cream over a nice tune?

stopped so suddenly we nearly crashed into the back of him.

'What?' I said. Bee nudged me and pointed.

'That,' she said.

Across the other side, there was a boy in a bright red

T-shirt. A boy with black curly hair. The boy was grinning.

'Fifty, what you doing?' shouted Copper Pie.

'Waiting for an audience,' he said. 'No point being brave without witnesses. That's why I sounded the horn. Worked, didn't it?'

I think Max caught up with us at exactly the moment Fifty let go of the top rung of the ladder and began the armpit-stretching journey across the water.

Mr Morris appeared when Fifty was on the third rung. He was wearing a fluffy blue dressing gown. The nurse person with the glasses was right behind him. Miss Walsh, who I hadn't seen all week, was next.

'We should stop that boy,' said Mr Morris.

Don't stop him, I wanted to say.

Miss Walsh opened her mouth but . . .

'Let's wait,' said Max. 'I think he wants a second chance.'

I counted the rungs – there were ten. Fifty was on number five, but he wasn't exactly whipping across. It's hard to hang by your arms, fine for howler monkeys but not great for humans. *Come on, Fifty.* He made rung six, but he was too slow. Everyone knows you have to make yourself go fast or it's too tiring. The longer you hang, the less likely you are to make it. He was stuck on six. His face was going red. And he wasn't grinning any more. He was going to fail, for the second time. As soon as I had that thought I knew I had to do something RIGHT AWAY. I grabbed the arm next to me, which happened to belong to Jonno, and headed for

Fifty. He might not be able to do it on his own, but he could it with our help.

'Good thinking, Keener,' said Jonno as we launched into the freezing cold river. It took a second to get over the shock. But in two seconds we were under Fifty's dangling legs, and then they weren't dangling, they were standing on a pair of shoulders (well one of mine and one of Jonno's). Fifty was going to make it, just not in quite the same way as everyone else.

Bee started clapping, a few people joined in, and then more. Fifty jumped off our shoulders, with the help of our bended knees, and on to the grassy bank. There was shouting and hollering and wild clapping. Everyone was for him, even though he still hadn't made the crossing on his own. Max came to the edge and slapped him on the back.

'Top try, Fifty.'

Fifty shrugged. 'Got halfway.'

'Six-tenths actually,' I said.

'Nerd,' said Copper Pie. (I do think being able to add up shouldn't necessarily qualify you as a nerd. Most people can do it.)

Max took Fifty's hand and held it high (well, as high as it would go) and said, 'This member of Team Tribe has just shown us that it's the things you find difficult that are worth the most. If you can swing over the monkey bars like a chimpanzee, like Copper Pie did, that's great, but it's not a challenge. You find out what a person's really made of when they're faced with something they'd rather *not* do.'

It was a good moment. No, not a good moment, a great moment. I glanced at Callum to check the sickly smile had been wiped off his face. Too right it had.

We walked back to the mess tent, hungry for breakfast. In the bacon queue Copper Pie turned to Fifty and said, 'It would've been a whole lot easier if you'd done it the first time.'

'No it wouldn't,' said Bee. 'This way Fifty got to be a hero. If he'd done the monkey bars first time like everyone else, he'd still just be Fifty – slightly small, bit of a show off.'

Fifty gave her a you're-not-a-nice-person look.

We were back to teasing, which meant we were back to normal, that was all that mattered. Tribe was back to normal. (And our reputation was restored.)

The Final Challenge

We had to pack up, and dismantle the tents. Max said the quicker we cleared the area, the sooner we'd get to play crab football and the longer we could play crab football for. Crab football is good. Even girls like crab football. We shoved everything in our bags, which wasn't easy because either the bags had shrunk or our stuff had swollen.

Team Tribe reported for football at the same time as Team GB so we were put down first on the play list. It was a tournament. Ten minutes per game. Winners play winners. Losers play losers. Blah blah. Max dragged two ancient goals out of a door next to the washrooms and we helped tent peg them down.

'OK. Your goalie can use hands, everyone else feet only.'

'Who's goalie?' I said.

'Not me,' said Bee. 'I'm going to be a striker.'

'Same,' said Fifty.

'I'll be goalie,' said Jonno.

'Sorted,' said Copper Pie. 'Let's practise.' He fetched one of the balls (lighter than a football, smaller than a beach ball), got down on all fours, tummy-side up . . . if you get what I mean, and started to dribble the ball.

I made my crab.

'Pass it to me.' He kicked me the ball. I missed and it went straight past. Lily picked it up.

'No hands, Lily,' said Bee. Lily threw the ball at Bee, who caught it.

'No hands, Bee.' She said back. Max blew a whistle.

'OK. Team GB versus Team Tribe. Get into positions. I suggest two at the front, two mid, one sweeper at the back and goalie. We'll start with a centre pass for Team GB.'

An interception by Bee gave us possession right away. We were off. She passed to Fifty, who kicked it straight ahead to no one. Copper Pie crab-sprinted after the ball, overtaking everyone else. A boy from Team GB had the ball but Copper Pie just ran into him, hooked the ball out from between his feet and shot at goal. The goalie stopped it with his knee, but the rebound landed at the feet of our redheaded football freak. Smack! Team Tribe score!

After ten minutes of utter humiliation (for them) the score was 13-0, all goals scored by you know who. That got us talking about the awards ceremony. *Maybe we'd be back in contention for the lead if we won the crab football?*

'We are so going to be top,' said Bee.

'We haven't even seen the other teams play yet,' said Jonno. I don't think anyone heard. They were already laughing about how sick Callum would be if Tribe triumphed again.

Our next match was against Alice's team, Flower Power, who'd beaten Hogwarts. We annihilated them, no problem, which put us in the semi-final against the Missiles. No way was Tribe going to lose to Callum and Jamie's team.

Except our magic feet (or rather Copper Pie's) deserted us in the third match. We were level at 3–3, sweating and desperate to score, and I for one was equally desperate to turn over into a more human position. My wrists were 'weak as a kitten', like Big Jim's.

'Sudden death from now on,' Max said. 'We're into extra time so we play golden goal, the first to score goes through to the final.'

There was a big crowd watching. It was our centre pass. Bee took it, passed back to Copper Pie. I think he was going to try and take it all the way but Callum and Jamie were on him. He tried to get rid of the ball to Fifty who was crabbing alongside but it deflected off Jamie and landed at the feet of another Missile, who lobbed it high in the air. We all watched it soar up and then loop down, bouncing right in front of Jonno, who totally misjudged everything and grabbed at thin air while the ball hopped into the goal behind him. Missiles win!

We were sick. Beaten by the team we most wanted not to be beaten by. We sat in a huddle, ignoring the other semi-final, and Copper Pie did a running commentary of our match and what we did wrong. I didn't listen. I thought about going home instead. We'd had a great time but I was looking forward to getting back to my room, particularly my hammock. There's something about swinging while you read that's really nice.

The camp horn sounded, announcing the final: Missiles versus Mountainboarders.

'Up you get,' said Bee. 'We need to make sure Ed and Marco pulverise the Missiles.'

'Too right,' said Lily.

'Same,' said Fifty.

We lined up and from when the second play began, we yelled our heads off. It was a good game. Both sides were fixed on winning. Copper Pie coached from the sideline. Callum did his usual hogging of the ball. There were loads of goals in all the other matches but this time – zilch. It was nearly full time when Marco messed up his pass and Callum got the ball, just feet from the goal. I shut my eyes, but the sound from the crowd told me the answer. Missiles had scored.

'COME ON, MOUNTAINBOARDERS!!!' Copper Pie nearly lost his tonsils. 'You've only got seconds to score.'

That was all they needed to hear. Marco crab-slid to steal the ball off Jamie, kicked it to Ed who did exactly what the Missiles did to us. He lobbed the ball sky-high, it landed and bounced right over the Missiles' goalie's head and dropped into the goal. 1–1.

'One more of the same,' shouted Copper Pie.

'Shut it, Ginge,' shouted Callum from the middle of the pitch.

'If you were less of a hog, your team'd stand a chance.'

Callum turned and took a couple of crab-steps towards Copper Pie. His face was red and sweaty and his blond fringe was stuck to his forehead. 'Don't call me Hog.'

Max could see there was something other than just the game going on. 'Come on, Callum. We're still playing here.'

Callum crabbed over to near where Jamie was waiting to do a kick from the sideline where the ball had gone out of play. The ball went straight to Callum's foot and stuck to it like superglue as Callum made his way up field.

'Tackle,' shouted Copper Pie.

Ed tackled, as directed, but Callum went through him, leaving only the goalie to beat.

But Marco came from nowhere, and as Callum took back his foot to welly the ball, Marco's whole leg sideswiped him, leaving Callum flat on his back. Marco didn't wait to assess the damage – he kicked the ball as hard as he could the other way. Another Mountainboarder scooped it up and aimed high – the ball flew into the corner of the net.

Whistle.

Mountainboarders win 2–1.

Brilliant result. If it couldn't be us, they were the next best. Copper Pie ran on to the pitch to slap a few backs. I stayed where I was, enjoying the sunshine and the furious look on Callum's face. He's not a good loser. Shame we weren't going to win the team award – that would ruin his day big time. I wondered who was going to win . . .

The Highwoods Awards Ceremony

Max, the nurse person, Mr Morris, Miss Walsh and two other adults that I hadn't seen before all stood at the entrance to the mess tent with a table in front of them. On the table were goodies – chocolates and more chocolates and jellybeans and more jellybeans. There was also a pile of yellow papers, and some white rolled-up ones.

'So, we come to the end of another successful camp at Highwoods,' said the nurse. 'And we like to finish off with a review of the highlights, before we go on to present the awards.'

She handed over to Max who gave quite a funny talk about all the activities, including our awesome raft building and the Mountainboarders' awesome crab-football playing. *Hurry up with the prizes,* I thought.

'So, we've got a few awards to hand out. The team in overall third place is . . . the Spiders.' There was clapping. 'They performed well in the quiz, did two cracking breakfast duties and collected more fuel for the fire than any other team.' He looked over at them. 'Come up here, Spiders.'

We clapped more. They trooped up – Zoe looked as pink in the face as I go, strawberry-jam pink. They got a certificate each (the yellow things) and a jar of jellybeans, and then Max picked up one of the white things, unrolled it and held it up. It was a photo of the Spiders on their raft, most of them half on and half off. Everyone cheered.

'And in second place, let's hear it for Flower Power, who designed an excellent raft, helped Miss Walsh make the camp cake, did an astonishing display of synchronised swimming in the sea and were the best all-girl team in the crab football.'

I had no idea they were any good, but then again their group was in the other half so we didn't see them much. Their photo was brilliant – they'd made a flower shape, using their bodyboards as petals, and they were lying on them in the sea. Cool. Alice grabbed the photo – no surprise there.

I had a rush of hope that we'd be first, I mean we won two legs of the assault course, and the quiz. Maybe the football didn't count . . .

'So, this year's camp champions are . . . the Mountainboarders. Top at crab football. Top at duck racing, and in Marco's case duck *embracing*.' He paused so everyone could laugh about the way Marco leapt in the water to congratulate his duck on winning, which they did. 'And for doing a *mountain* of washing-up.' Mad clapping. Marco started bowing. Ed copied. They were the centre of attention. They got jellybeans *and* chocolate, and the picture Max held up was of the six of them all holding on to their winning duck. I wished we could have had a photo.

I felt a bit disappointed. We were winning after the quiz, but didn't even end up in the top three. I wasn't cross with Fifty – I know he didn't fail on purpose, but I wished he had managed the monkey bars. I wasn't cross with Jonno either – anyone of us could have let that goal in, but if he'd judged the bounce a bit better the story might have been completely different. We might have been prize winners.

'Now, we have three extra individual awards for noteworthy performances.' I tried to think if I'd done anything noteworthy. Nothing came to mind. 'A jar of jelly beans is awarded to Roddy for offering to organise the litter collection and making sure it was done every evening.' (I didn't know there *was* a litter collection.) Everyone clapped while Roddy got his sweets. 'And two monster bars of chocolate for two other helpful members of camp, who showed both cooperation with other teams and a keen sense of loyalty to their own.' I looked around to see who the loyal, cooperative, helpful kids were. *Probably girls*, I thought. *Tidying their tents and doing each other's hair.*

'Jonno.' Everyone turned to look at him. He stood up and shrugged as if to say, 'I don't know what I did to deserve it.' I didn't know either. Max smiled at him.

'And Keener.' Me!!! Everyone turned to look at me. Instant raspberry face. I got up but kept my eyes on my knees.

'Keener and Jonno helped the other teams get the hang of bodyboarding. Jonno did some useful lugging of wood with the Spiders. And this morning they both stepped in to help a member of their team make an unscheduled crossing of the river.' Max held up a photo of Fifty standing with one foot on my shoulder and one on Jonno's.

I waited for Jonno to go up and get the prizes together, but he said, 'Come on, Tribers. All for one and one for all.'

So Bee, Copper Pie, Fifty, Jonno and I all went up together. (Bee tried to drag Lily too, but she didn't want to come because she's not a Triber.) I took the photo and carried it back to where we were sitting. Fifty grabbed the chocolate before Copper Pie had a chance – Jonno didn't get a look in. Not that he cared.

Everyone got a certificate to take home and show their parents, and on each one there was a comment but they were mostly rubbish like *A good team player* – that was on Jonno's, and *Tried hard at Highwoods* – mine. Whatever. I was too busy staring at our photo. We were all in it. Even though the focus was on Fifty, Jonno and me, the photographer had caught the back of Copper Pie's head and the side of Bee's.

I knew exactly where it was going to hang – the wall of the Tribehouse. We did the fist of friendship. Did we care that we hadn't won the best team? Or even made the top three?

Nope. Not one bit. We'd triumphed at camp, the photo showed it. We'd done it the Tribe way, that's all.

tribers.co.uk

Find out more about the Tribers online!